It wasn't a ████████ **she told herse** ████████ **s she glossed h** ████████ **check in the mirror.**

She had to keep her head tonight, had to see how things went tonight before she did anything. She almost doubled up then, stunned at the possibilities her mind lurched to, for he made her feel rash, dizzy, *want.*

Zander, too, smiled as he looked into the mirror.

Tonight was such an unexpected treat.

He had enjoyed flirting with Charlotte on the phone, getting her to open up a little, and though last night he had intended to loosen her tongue with fine wine, the stakes were raised now. He had not anticipated the rare beauty of her—that she might live up to the voice he had enjoyed these past weeks.

Now he wanted her.

Tonight, he would have Charlotte in his bed.

The Secrets of Xanos

Two brothers alike in charisma and power;
separated at birth and seeking revenge…

Nico—the good twin

Brought up to be a good Greek boy, he's always felt like
an outsider. He's turned his back on his parents' fortune
to become one of Xanos's most powerful exports.

Nothing will stand in the way of him discovering
the truth, until he stumbles upon a virgin bride…an
encounter that has shameful consequences….

Zander—the forgotten twin

He took his chances on the streets rather than spend
another moment under his cruel father's roof.
He's pulled himself up by the bootstraps and is unrivaled
in business—and the bedroom!

He wants the best people around him, and Charlotte is
the best personal assistant! But she works for his rival…
unless he can tempt her over to the dark side.

Carol Marinelli

AN INDECENT PROPOSITION

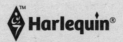

TORONTO   NEW YORK   LONDON
AMSTERDAM   PARIS   SYDNEY   HAMBURG
STOCKHOLM   ATHENS   TOKYO   MILAN   MADRID
PRAGUE   WARSAW   BUDAPEST   AUCKLAND

Recycling programs
for this product may
not exist in your area.

ISBN-13: 978-0-373-13059-7

AN INDECENT PROPOSITION

All about the author...
Carol Marinelli

CAROL MARINELLI finds writing a bio rather like writing her New Year's resolutions. Oh, she'd love to say that since she wrote the last one, she now goes the gym regularly and doesn't stop for coffee and cake and gossip afterward; that she's incredibly organized; and that she writes for a few productive hours a day after tidying her immaculate house and taking a brisk walk with the dog.

The reality is Carol spends an inordinate amount of time day dreaming about dark, brooding men and exotic places (research), which doesn't leave too much time for the gym, housework or anything that comes in between. And her most productive writing hours happen to be in the middle of the night, which leaves her in a constant state of bewildered exhaustion.

Originally from England, Carol now lives in Melbourne, Australia. She adores going back to the UK for a visit—actually, she adores going anywhere for a visit—and constantly (expensively) strives to overcome her fear of flying. She has three gorgeous children who are growing up so fast (too fast—they've just worked out that she lies about her age!) and keep her busy with a never-ending round of homework, sports and friends coming over.

A nurse and a writer, Carol writes for the Harlequin® Presents and Medical Romance lines and is passionate about both. She loves the fast-paced, busy setting of a modern hospital, but every now and then admits it's bliss to escape to the glamorous, alluring world of her heroes and heroines in her Harlequin Presents novels. A bit like her real life actually!

Other titles by Carol Marinelli available in eBook:

Harlequin Presents®

*The Secrets of Xanos

CHAPTER ONE

SHE looked forward to his calls far more than she should.

Charlotte knew that.

She should be distant, professional, polite when dealing with this powerful man—but the sound of his voice, the way he paused after her comment, the way she knew that he was smiling at something she had said made Charlotte's toes curl as she lay in her bed.

There had been several calls now. The first had started with Zander terse and abrupt. His Greek accent had been confusing for Charlotte, so much so that she'd actually thought it was her boss Nico in a bad mood. Her phone had rung at six a.m. and it had taken a moment to register that the caller was, in fact, the elusive property owner that she had been chasing on Nico's behalf. It was not one of his lawyers, or the sour PA she was more used to dealing with, but the very man himself.

'This is Zander,' he had snapped to her fuddled brain. 'I thought you wanted to speak with me—it would seem that I was mistaken.'

He had been about to ring off—clearly irritated that she hadn't instantly recognised him—but knowing how badly Nico would take it if she lost this point of contact, Charlotte had stammered out an apology. 'I'm s-sorry for the confusion. It's wonderful to have you return my call.' She hadn't added a sarcastic *finally* to her sentence, though she'd been tempted; instead, she'd glanced at her bedside clock. "It's just that it's six a.m. here.'

There had been a pause, a lengthy one, and though certainly not conciliatory his voice had been a touch less brusque when next he spoke. 'I thought it was eight. You are in Athens, no? Xanos?'

'London.' Charlotte had dragged herself up to sitting in bed.

'You are Charlotte Edwards? Nico Eliades's PA?'

'Yes, but I'm based in London.'

And then, most unexpectedly, came an apology.

'Forgive me. I am in Australia…I just assumed when I worked out the times that, like your boss, you would be in Greece. I will call you back during office hours.'

'There's no need,' Charlotte said hurriedly, not wanting to tell Nico the elusive Zander had finally called and that she had been too groggy to deal with it. 'Don't ring off—I'm up now. Well, not up…'

Oh, dear!

There was a long pause, from both parties. Charlotte cringed because, far from coming across as an efficient PA, she had made it clear she was lying in bed. Zander, well, his pause, followed by a light huskiness to his voice, made her blush further, and not because she was cringing. It was for other reasons entirely.

'Do you want to get a coffee?' he asked. 'I will call back.'

'No, I'm fine…' Charlotte lied, reaching for a pen, determined to be ready whatever figures he flung at her, to be poised and fully engaged. Even if she was desperate to go to the loo, to check on her mum, and, yes, grab a coffee, she would not show it. Then he spoke again and, on a cold London morning, somehow his voice seemed to caress her. Somehow the elusive billionaire spoke not at her but to her.

'Charlotte, I will call you back in five minutes. Go and get a coffee and bring it back to bed—and then we can talk.'

She was about to correct him, for only Nico called her Charlotte in her work. Ms Edwards kept things rather more formal—instilled immediate distance—but it seemed petty to correct Zander when she may have already appeared rude. Whether it sounded efficient or not, she answered with the truth.

'That would be lovely, Mr…?'

'Zander,' came his brief response before he promptly rang off.

This was how it had started.

Yes, she looked forward to his calls far more than she should—their early morning chats had become a routine. He would call at some ungodly hour, talk for a brief moment and then hang up; she would make coffee, bring it back to bed, wait for the ring of her work phone and then listen to his rich, deep voice. She would write down the messages to relay to Nico, dispense with work, and then *they* would talk.

Not much.

Just a little more than perhaps she should.

'So you don't actually work with Nico?' Zander had probed one Sunday night. The unexpected timing had surprised her, though, of course, Charlotte realised, it was Monday morning there. She was huddled under the sheets, the weather filthy outside, the sound of rain on the windows and his voice keeping her warm.

'I work for him.'

'But not alongside him.'

'I work from home,' Charlotte explained. 'Nico travels a lot and I organise things from this end.'

'And do you enjoy it?'

And she hesitated, not for long, just a brief second. 'I love it.'

Which she did, Charlotte told herself and then told herself again. It was a wonderful job, but that was all it was to her—a job rather than a passion, a means to an end rather than the career she had once loved. As a child, 'an international flight attendant' had been her unwavering response when asked what she wanted to be when she grew up. She had studied language at school, and beyond, had applied for and worked for her first airline of choice, been swiftly promoted through the ranks to become a lead attendant. How she longed to be in the air now with her first-class passengers, taking the flight crew their breakfast and lingering in the cockpit at forty thousand feet in the air as they flew towards dawn.

'Don't you miss the company?' he asked, and his question was so direct, so right on the mark she couldn't answer for a second, and stupidly there were tears in her eyes because, hell, yes, she missed company, missed so badly not just the flying but the social aspect too. 'Of course, it would be perfect,' Zander mused to the silence, 'if you have young children.'

'Oh, I don't have children,' she said without thinking, and there was a beat where she realised his question hadn't been so idle, that Zander was gauging her, and it made her feel warm. 'You?'

'Absolutely not. I'm far too irresponsible.' The way that he said it had Charlotte biting on her bottom lip. She chose not to tell him that she nursed her mother at home, and that Amanda's Alzheimer's was worsening. Chose not to tell him that, far from hard, working for Nico was the only work she could do. That being available all hours on the computer or phone, with the handsome wage Nico paid, meant that she could keep the promise her mother had begged for and look after her at home.

'So?' Zander did not let it rest. 'Do you miss the company?'

'Not at all.' She lied, because it was safer. Lied, because if she told him the truth she might just break down. So she told him about lunches with friends and cocktails on Friday, told him about the Charlotte she had once been when she had travelled the world for a living.

'I am reluctant to sell this land.' He turned the conversation back to work. 'Your boss is very insistent. He wants the jetty, of course, because then that entire stretch of cove would be his.'

She said nothing. She was not there for discussion, or for negotiation. Her job was to pass messages on to Nico.

'Have you seen it?' Zander asked. 'Have you been to Xanos?'

And here she could not stay silent, for she had been there, just for a day, and just the once, and she could see absolutely why her boss wanted a slice of it. 'I have and it's completely stunning.' It was—an exclusive, private retreat for the rich and famous. Nico had, for an extremely inflated price, bought from Zander an undeveloped house but, newly married and used to the best, he wanted more for his new wife and son. For weeks now his main focus had been on securing the neighbouring land; however, Zander was reluctant to sell.

'Did you put my lease option to him?'

'I did,' Charlotte said, 'but he's not interested. He really wants to speak with you himself.'

'I rather prefer speaking with you.'

He didn't go far, but it was far enough to have Charlotte blushing, the little hint that he enjoyed their conversations as much as she.

'I should get up,' Zander said.

'Oh.' And she closed her eyes for always he sounded

so *dressed*, so together, she had assumed him at a desk, but it made her toes curl to think he was lying in bed too. 'I thought you were at work.'

'I am,' he said, and she could feel his seductive smile even if she could not see it. 'I can work just as hard on my back.'

He did smile then, though she could not see it. He smiled because he heard her. Heard her inhale as she did now and then, not through her nose but with a catch in her throat. Over the last days it was a sound he had come to crave —so much so that he had dropped his date at her home last night rather than bring her to his, choosing the pleasure of Charlotte's voice to wake up to.

'You sound tired, you're in bed early.'

'I am.' And it was far easier to say she had been at a wedding the previous night than up at two a.m., chasing her mother through dark streets, trying to persuade her to come back to the house. It was easier by far to tell this glamorous, exotic man, whom she had never met, that her life was a little more fab than drab, to paint a picture, safe in the knowledge they would probably never meet. With Zander on the end of the phone, for a few precious moments she got to live the life she invented.

'Was it a good wedding?'

'It was lovely,' Charlotte replied, thinking of her boss's wedding a few weeks ago, which she had organised but not attended. 'It went off without a hitch.'

'Was it very formal? Did you wear a hat?' His voice was so low she had to concentrate to hear it, but in the nicest of ways. 'I did,' Charlotte said, and that was a complete and utter lie, for Nico's wedding had been tiny and informal, held on the beach of his bayside property on the Greek Island of Xanos, with just a couple of witnesses. Charlotte played her game, closed her eyes and imagined, escaped for a little while, safe in the knowledge she would never meet Zander. 'Though it was a bit windy in the photos. I was worried I might lose it...'

'And do you have plans for tomorrow?'

'Just out for lunch with friends,' Charlotte said, wishing badly it were true, but long lunches with girlfriends were a thing of the past now. Still, it was nice to lie here and dream, nicer still to be in bed talking to Zander and know he was doing the same. 'Okay. Tell your boss I am still considering things.' It was Zander who wrapped up the conversation, but at the same time he opened up her heart. 'He is lucky to have you.'

'Lucky?' Charlotte frowned into the phone.

'Were it not for how much I enjoy speaking with his PA, I would have turned him down.'

And even if Charlotte glowed inside, she reined it in, for her boss was Nico.

'You're not just stringing him along?'

'Charlotte...' His voice was very even, perhaps a little precise. 'I have better things to do with my time than string your boss along. I was ringing to refuse his offer that first day—it was you that made me reconsider.'

He rang off then, and Charlotte lay there, replaying the conversation in her mind, trying to tell herself she was being ridiculous. He was making conversation, that was all, flirting as he probably did with most women. For maybe the hundredth time she pulled over her laptop, her intention to find out all she could about him.

To see him.

But as she had so many times before, Charlotte stopped herself.

His voice, the way he said her name, the way sometimes he *asked* about her, the way he made her feel… she didn't want it to fade, didn't want to find out he was some overweight married man, flirting on the phone. Didn't want this feeling to end.

She dreamt of him, heard his deep, rich voice over and over, and actually awoke with a smile on her face. Getting up, Charlotte looked into the mirror. Her long, honey-blonde hair needed a serious trim, her baggy pyjamas were unfit for male eyes and all she looked was exhausted, nothing like the glamorous woman Zander thought she was. As Charlotte walked into her mother's bedroom, the smell of wet sheets had her close her eyes for a moment. She opened them to her mother's vacant stare.

'Morning, Mum.' As usual, Charlotte got no response, so she tried in her mother's native language, which she had reverted to almost completely now. *'Bonjour, maman.'* Still there was no response. 'Let's get you up for your shower.'

It was so much easier said than done. Charlotte was thumped on the side of her head, scratched on her arm, told to *'Casse-toi'*, and the screams from her mother as she washed her would, had the neighbours not known better, have had them calling the police, for it sounded as if Amanda was being attacked.

Still, it got done and even if Charlotte was still in her pyjamas, at least her mum was bathed, scented and dressed and finally sitting down in her chair in the lounge.

'We could go for a walk on the beach.' Her mother finally spoke, as Charlotte fed her a soft-boiled egg, mashed in with butter, in the hope of adding a few calories, for it wasn't just her mother's mind that was fading away. But even if her words sounded lucid, even if it sounded like a normal conversation, it was, of course, otherwise—they were miles from the beach. But it was her mother's favourite place and when she spoke of the beach, it was always in English, as if she were truly remembering times when she had taken Charlotte there as a child.

'We will,' Charlotte said. 'We could feed the seagulls, maybe?' And she saw her mother smile, saw her eyes and face light up, and even if they would never get to the beach again, would never feed the seagulls together again, her mother's smile was worth the fib.

And it was worth it, Charlotte told herself as she dragged herself through another week. Worth putting her life on hold to take care of her mother, although deep down she knew it couldn't go on much longer.

That *she* couldn't go on much longer.

But, then, like a lifeline came the call.

Mid-afternoon, and not at all his usual time, her heart leapt when she saw that it was Zander. She answered with a smile, anticipating the summer of his words, except his tone was brusque, businesslike.

'Could you pass on a message to Nico?'

'Of course.' She glanced at the clock and tried to work out the times. It must be four in the morning where Zander was.

'I am going to be in Xanos next week. I fly in late Sunday and my schedule is very full, but if you can arrange a meeting with your boss, I have a small window at eight a.m. on Monday. We are moving into the next stage of the development in the coming weeks. I want to discuss with him, before the purchase goes ahead, our plans for that area. He might not be so keen and I don't want him wasting my time later with petitions.'

'I'll let him know.' She waited, waited for the conversation to change as it always did, to slip back to where they spoke about them—but it didn't. Zander rang off and Charlotte rang Nico and relayed the message, but as she hung up, she felt like crying. Knew that once Zander met with Nico, her part in this would be over—that the brief escape his calls had bought would finally come to an end. When Nico rang a few moments later she had to force herself back into business mode.

'How good are you with Greek planning permission laws?'

'Are there such things?' She smiled into the phone, but it faded as Nico spoke on.

'Exactly. Anyway, I've got Paulo onto it, but I'm going to need you in Xanos next week.'

'Me?' Charlotte blinked and then wished she hadn't

for in that instant her mother wandered out to the hall; Charlotte walked briskly, catching Amanda as she fiddled with the catch on the front door.

'Do you really need me there?' It wasn't a no, but it was as close as she dared.

'I wouldn't ask otherwise. I'd like you to visit a couple of homes for me, go through some records...' Since Nico had found out he was adopted, Charlotte had been helping him to find his birth mother, but it had all been through telephone calls and online. She had chosen not to tell him about her problems with her own mother: PAs dealt with their boss's problems, not the other way around. He'd asked her to join him in Xanos a couple of months ago, but that had just been for a day. The carer she had hired had informed her on her return that her mother required too high a level of care. For any future trips Amanda would need to be cared for in a home. 'Is there a problem?' She knew he was frowning. Nico was not a man used to hearing the word 'no', and certainly not from his PA.

'Of course not.' Charlotte swallowed. 'I just need to sort out a few things at this end, but I'll do my best to be there on Monday.'

'Actually...' Nico sounded distracted. 'If you can get in earlier, perhaps the weekend, we can go over a few things. Book in at Ravels and ring me when you get here.'

'Sure,' Charlotte said to thin air, for Nico had already rung off. She had to speak to him when she saw him, had to somehow tell her formidable boss that travel was practically impossible. But what if he insisted? Charlotte closed her eyes at the prospect. She needed this job, needed the wage, needed the flexibility working from home provided—maybe she would have to factor in an occasional trip.

She already had a list of nursing homes drawn up. Charlotte had visited several, riddled with guilt each and every time, for her mother had, on her diagnosis, pleaded with Charlotte to never put her in a home. Now she rang them, asking if there were any respite beds available, her anxiety increasing as she worked her way through the list and each time the response was the same. Far more notice was required.

Finally she found one. A resident had died overnight, and there was a spot available. It felt wrong to be relieved, wrong to be packing up her mother's things, wrong to be driving a distressed Amanda to the place she dreaded most in the world.

'It's just for a few days, Mum.'

'Please…' Amanda sobbed. 'Please don't leave me. Please.'

'I have to go to work, Mum.' Charlotte was crying too. 'I promise, it's just for a little while.'

All it felt was wrong—to sit in the chair at the beauty parlour and be waxed and manicured, to have foils put in her thick blonde hair. Wrong to think of her mother sobbing in a home as she transformed herself back into the glamorous flight attendant Nico had hired.

But there was a flutter of excitement there too as

she pulled out her old wardrobe and packed in her efficient way.

And there was that pit-in-the-stomach thrill as she drove the familiar route to Heathrow airport, saw the jets coming in and heard the high-pitched roar as they took off.

And then, as she sat in her seat, as the plane lifted off the ground and up to the sky, as she looked at the flight attendant facing her and wished she could be her, there was that moment at take-off she would forever adore, the surreal moment where the plane seemed to quiet and you gathered your thoughts. And only then did it actually dawn on her.

She was going to meet Zander.

CHAPTER TWO

ATHENS had been as grey as London, but flying towards Xanos it was as if the clocks had been rewound to autumn. Certainly it would not be as warm as the summer, but the sky was as blue, as was the ocean, and Xanos lay stretched out in the distance, a vivid tapestry of greens and browns. The vineyards laced the mountains and the stunning hotel development stood on the foreshore, gorgeous buildings carved into the cliff side, glittering blue infinity pools that matched the blue jewel of the ocean. She could not wait to land, to sink her feet in the golden sands and to drink in Xanos.

The seaplane came in, not beside the small jetty her boss craved to own but to the newly built, rather more sophisticated one. A ramp made disembarking far easier than it had been the last time Charlotte had visited Xanos, and because anyone who stayed at Ravels must be someone, though she would have loved to, she was not expected to make the short walk from the jetty to the hotel. Instead, she was swallowed by a huge car and driven the short distance into the development, escorted to check in and told that her bags would be taken straight to her room.

Usually she was not intimated by grand surroundings. She had worked long enough with the airline and later with Nico to sample fine hotels and luxury travel, but, though she did her best not to show it, Charlotte found this hotel somewhat overwhelming. Some of the guests who moved through the foyer she recognised from the magazines she devoured. A huge elevator was situated beside a grand staircase, separated by a fountain. There were lavish floral displays at every turn, wealth and opulence in every view; it was hard to believe the hotel had just been in operation for a few short months.

Checking in went smoothly; there was a message from Paulo, Nico's lawyer in Greece, asking her to contact him, and Charlotte declined the receptionist's offer of a booking in the restaurant. She would rather eat alone in her room. Swipe card in hand, she wandered through the hotel, not quite brave enough to have a drink at the bar; instead, she headed for her room, bouncing on the huge king-sized bed and revelling for a guilty moment in the feeling that tonight she would not have to sleep with one ear open in case her mother awoke, that she had a little time to herself.

Still, she was here to work, so she rang Nico and got his voicemail. She told him she had arrived and then she rang Paulo too.

'I'm unable to get hold of Nico,' Paulo said. 'I want to speak with him before this meeting on Monday.'

'I've just left a message.'

'Well, if you do get hold of him, make sure he speaks with me. He says that he doesn't want me present on Monday, but I don't want him speaking with this developer without me—he's bad news.'

'Really?' Normally she would not pursue the conversation, would simply pass the message on, but she was far too interested in the elusive Zander, too curious about the voice she had heard on the end of the phone, to let the opportunity to know more pass by. 'Zander certainly seems inflexible, but…'

Paulo said something in Greek that Charlotte couldn't decipher and then he translated. 'It's a saying here on Xanos—this man is someone who would sell their own mother to the highest bidder. Nico needs to watch out—make sure you have him ring me.'

Paulo was always cautious, Charlotte told herself as she hung up the phone. It was his job to be cautious, she consoled herself. Anyway, she was spending far too much time thinking about a man she had never even met, a man she had spoken to only on the phone, but she didn't want him to be a man like the one Paulo was describing. She wanted him to be every bit as gorgeous as the one she had secretly imagined.

Charlotte stepped out onto the balcony; she could hear a couple from the suite beside her, though couldn't see them because of privacy walls, but their conversation was so exotic and glamorous it was heaven to eavesdrop while she looked out to the beach, to the azure water and gorgeous sands. For a moment she almost felt back in her old life, except there were no colleagues to meet up with, no one to explore the island with, no one to lie with her by the pool, as so often she had.

An uneasy feeling seemed to pool in her throat, tasting of bitterness and martyrdom—the food she had been fed by her mother throughout her childhood. And that was the very last thing she wanted.

She needed to think, really think about her future, and even if the neighboring conversation was intriguing, the beach beckoned more and Charlotte headed inside. She pulled on a simple shift dress, light cardigan and sandals, wanting to catch the last of the evening sun.

Still, even though she was miles from home, even though it was a relief to have a night to herself and the secret pleasure of finally coming face to face with Zander on Monday, as she walked along the golden sands of Xanos, her thoughts turned to her mum. Amanda would have loved it here. Their yearly holidays through Charlotte's childhood were perhaps her most treasured of memories, for it was the only time she had ever really seen her mother happy; the only time Amanda had seemed at peace instead of bitter about the career she had forgone and the lover who, when Amanda had found out she was pregnant, had spurned her instead of facing up to his responsibilities.

How could Charlotte do it to her—put her in a home because it made life easier? Even all these years on, Charlotte nursed guilt for her childish selfishness, for the way she had idolised her absent father, not aware of the sacrifices her mother had made. Oh, the rows and tears that had come from her brought a sting of shame today. But once a year they had cast it aside, walked along Camber Sands or Beachy Head and, without fail, her mother would buy an extra portion of fries each evening, a ten-minute indulgence where they'd feed the seagulls and laugh and whoop as the gathered birds went wild.

There was Nico.

She looked up from her dreams and saw reality: her boss skimming stones in the water. It caught her by surprise, why she could not fathom for Nico lived here now—just along from this stretch of beach was his private residence. Something about him made her start. There was purpose to him, not idle relaxation as his wrist flicked the smooth, flat stones but an anger almost. She carried on walking, though she considered turning around, pretending she hadn't seen him, for so dark were his features, so deep his concentration, she wondered if he and his wife Constantine had just had a row. Still, it would be worse if he saw her turning and thought she was ignoring him, and she did need to pass Paulo's message on so, pretending she had not noticed his dark mood, she walked purposefully towards him, smiling as she called his name.

'Nico!' she called. 'I've been trying to ring you...' And then he turned around and her breath held in her lungs as she realised that, though he looked like him, though it surely was him, somehow the man that had turned to her call was not Nico. She could not explain it; the only thing she could liken it to was, years ago, as a

small child she had lost her mother in a department store
and a few panicked minutes later had rushed towards
the familiar beige coat and tugged on it, had looked up
at her mum and recoiled as she'd realised that it was not
her, that the eyes that frowned at her had not been her
mother's. The feeling was back, was there in her chest
now, as her familiar greeting was met with a stranger's
stare. 'Sorry.' She walked backwards for a few steps.
'My mistake…'

She wanted to turn and run, it was her first instinct,
she wanted to run, for her head was a mass of jumbled
thoughts, but instead she walked quickly, desperate to
get back to the hotel, to think, to talk to Nico, to find
out just what the hell was going on.

'Slow down.' His footsteps were muffled by the
sand, but still she heard them, could feel him as he
drew closer, jumped with the shock of contact as his
hand closed around her shoulder and spun her around.
'Why are you running?'

She turned to eyes that were black, blacker than
Nico's, to a face that appeared in every detail to come
from the same canvas as Nico's except the brush had
been dipped in an ink that was darker; the hand that had
created this masterpiece just a touch heavier than the
one that had made the other. His hair was longer, his
bone structure more severe, but it was his mouth that
drew her eyes for a second, a mouth that was heavy and
sensual, with beautifully white teeth that smiled a smile
that contradicted the bore of his gaze.

'I made a mistake…' She was far too confused to think logically. 'I thought you were someone else.'

'You thought I was Nico?' This was so not how he had planned it. Zander knew he had taken a risk walking on the beach, but being cooped in the hotel was driving him crazy. At the last minute he had changed his plans and flown in early, but it had been a mistake, for already there was a buzz at the hotel. He had checked in under a different name, wanting to see how the hotel ran when the staff were unaware the owner was in residence, but the curious looks told him that Nico was a regular. From the way this woman had approached, the fact she had been trying to ring Nico, Zander knew he had only moments to act to prevent his cover being blown. He wanted his moment on Monday, wanted to see Nico's reaction at first hand, and now he had to convince this woman, this stranger, not to tell him. Somehow he had to win her trust quickly, which was no trouble at all for a man like Zander, who could have any woman eating out of his hand in a matter of moments.

He smiled but his heart was not in it, though surely not a soul on earth could tell, for he had for so long perfected his routine. He looked deep into her eyes and focused on the glittering blue and his hand that was still on her wrist held her more loosely now, but the pulse that leaped beneath his fingers told him that she was in shock and it raced again when next he spoke.

'I am Nico's twin.'

'Twin?' She almost laughed at the ridiculousness of

her response, for of course he was his twin, except she hadn't even known that Nico had one.

'I'm Zander.' And from her blush when he said his name, from the slight catch in her throat, he recognised her. His weekend retreat suddenly became a lot more interesting, a lot more pleasurable perhaps? 'You must be Charlotte.' He smiled and it was deadly; it was a smile that had the hairs on her neck rise in strange response, made her arm pull back from his fingers, from the left hand that had shot out to grab her, when Nico would have used his right. 'Finally we meet.'

'You're Zander.' Her eyes flew away from his intense gaze as she wrestled with mortification—for if their dealings had already been a touch inappropriate, they were far more so now. It had been her boss's twin that she had flirted with.

Oh, and they had been flirting!

'I didn't know Nico even had a twin...' She could not think with him looking at her, could not be in his space. She stepped back a little, moved her eyes from the intensity of his gaze, back to his mouth, but she could not concentrate by looking there, so she looked downwards—to clothes that could never be described as casual, for there was luxury in every thread. The silk and cashmere black jumper billowed in the wind to give a blatant outline of his chest, the charcoal grey linen trousers rested low on narrow hips—there was no escape from his beauty. Even as she searched lower she was met with naked feet, the olive of his skin a contrast to the pale sand, and she wanted to get away from him, wanted the beach to be empty, wanted to get back to the safety of her thoughts and a walk that was gentle and aimless, instead of the confrontation with him.

'Neither does Nico,' Zander said. 'On Monday I plan to surprise him.' He must have seen the flare of worry in her eyes, for he moved swiftly to assure her, 'I am hoping that the surprise will be a pleasant one…' He sensed her doubt, knew that her instinct was to flee, and he did not want her spoiling all he had planned, did not want her running to Nico with her tales, but also… He looked down at the pale cream shift dress and the long slender arm he had a moment ago been holding, then up to the face that was just as pleasing as the voice he had dealt with in recent times, to the blonde hair that the wind whipped around her face and, yes, he wanted time with her, wanted to *meet* the voice that had entranced him, for on Monday, when he had said his piece, when he had wreaked his revenge, for sure, Charlotte would want nothing to do with him.

'I can't believe this.' She was completely stunned. 'Does this mean Nico has found his…?' She stopped herself from asking further. It was certainly not her business to probe into her boss's private life, and Nico gave little away. He had told her, more than a year ago, his suspicions that he was, in fact, adopted, but only so that she could be of assistance in researching his history. Though Nico was actively looking for his birth mother, not once had he mentioned that he had a twin—and an identical one too. She knew she had to speak with him, to get away from Zander and speak with Nico, but there was something that needed to be addressed.

'You knew when you spoke to me.' Her voice was accusing, which was ridiculous perhaps for he owed her nothing, but somehow she felt betrayed. 'I should go back…' There were so many questions and she must not look to him for answers. She plastered on a smile, pretended she was not perturbed, and tried to walk nonchalantly away from him.

'Stay,' Zander said.

'I have things to prepare, I have work to do…'

'Surely you have questions?'

She did, so very many, but surely the answers should come from Nico. Perhaps Zander sensed where her loyalties lay, and in that moment the battle was on—he wanted her loyalty, wanted to take everything from his brother, and Charlotte seemed a very good place to start.

'Let us just enjoy the evening,' he said. 'There is no harm surely in walking. Perhaps we could have a seat at the beach café and watch the sunset.'

Would it be rude to refuse?

Would Nico scold her on Monday for snubbing his brother?

'Or…' he sensed an opening '…we could just walk?'

She gave a hesitant nod. Her guard firmly up, she walked tentatively alongside him, determined to say nothing that might compromise Nico until she was sure what was going on.

'Are you enjoying the hotel?' Zander asked, and she remembered he owned it, that the man beside her owned the very ground they were walking on. She knew then the true might of this man.

'It's wonderful.'

'He was a hard man to find.' It was Zander who broke the tense silence; it was he who spoke of his brother. '*His* name is the one that is different.'

She said nothing to that.

'You like your job?' Zander changed track.

'Of course.' He heard her terse response and could only admire her restraint, for surely she must have a thousand questions, but he watched as she kept them in. He wanted her to speak of his brother, so he paved the way and spoke first about himself.

'I love it here.' The words choked in his throat, for he could not loathe the place more, but when she glanced up at him, Zander made sure he was smiling. 'Always it was my dream to come back...' He looked at the luxurious properties he'd had carved into the cliffs and hills of Xanos and she followed his gaze.

'Where was your house?' She could not help but ask, wondered for a mad moment if it was the house Nico lived in now, but he motioned vaguely to the middle of the development. 'Where is the one you grew up in?'

'Where the hotel is.' He saw her tiny frown. 'It was unsalvageable.' He chose not to tell her it had been the first property he had had knocked down, that he had stood with the best champagne in his hand in his office in Australia, and cheered silently as the bulldozer had set to work. Knowing that his family home was being destroyed had been the only moment of pleasure Xanos had given him.

'You like the beach?'

He saw that she relaxed a little at the less loaded question. 'I love it,' Charlotte admitted. 'Not swimming or anything…' She smiled, a real smile, the first since she had realised who she was speaking to, and he watched her blue eyes brighten, her mouth spread, and he wanted to see more of the same. 'Just walking, thinking…' Her eyes roamed the horizon. 'Remembering…' He wondered what. Perhaps romantic walks with Nico before he'd taken a wife, but her voice broke into his thoughts. 'We always holidayed at the beach,' Charlotte said. 'When I was younger.'

He heard her pensive pause and let it be, had learnt so very well how to deal with women, how to get them to unbend, how to win their trust. There was none more skilled at it than he. So brilliant was his technique that it left every woman stunned and breathless when his true nature was revealed, when the man who had listened so intently, had supposedly cared, just dismissed all they had briefly shared.

He was at his dangerous best now, a small question here, an insightful observation there, and as they strolled with seemingly little purpose Charlotte spoke more easily. As a seagull ducked and swooped at a piece of paper, she laughed. Another bird joined it and then another, furious screeches of protest when there was no food to be found.

'Poor things.'

'Poor things?' Zander gave a wry laugh. 'I can ensure for my guests many things, but a seagull-free beach would be the icing on the cake.'

'I love them.' And she laughed and then, because it was safer than talking about Nico, she told him about her long-ago walks with her mother on their holidays, how they had fed the gulls, how it had been a great end to their days.

They walked, five, maybe ten minutes more. The beach café was serving cocktails but they walked past all that to a place more secluded, away from the sand of the beach to the rocky coves around it. Charlotte, calm beside him, was forced to concentrate more on her step than her words.

'How long have you worked for Nico?'

'Nearly two years now,' Charlotte said, and he saw her tense, saw that she sensed perhaps he was fishing, but he worked carefully around that.

'And before that?' He tried to guess at her age, mid-twenties he gauged, which was very young to be an assistant to a man like Nico Eliades, but he was quite sure his brother had not hired her purely for her business skills. 'Did you do business studies?'

'Oh, no…' She shook her head. 'I never intended to be a PA—I was a flight attendant. International.' She added. 'That's how I met him.'

It galled Zander, but he did not show it.

'On a flight?'

Charlotte nodded. 'I recognised him back at the hotel I was booked into—he was having trouble being understood. We were in Japan and, unusually for that hotel, the staff member he was dealing with spoke very poor English, so I stepped in.'

'You speak Japanese?'

She held her finger and thumb a tiny space a part. 'A little. And my mother's French, so I can get by there too. Oh, and I can speak a little…*Mía glóssa then íne poté arketí.*' He smiled as she told him in his own language that one language was never enough. 'I love learning languages, it's my hobby. I'm studying now… Anyway, Nico was having trouble changing his flight…' And Zander had to force himself to remember that it was Nico he was trying to find out about, for instead he wanted to know more about her. He wanted to know about her life before Nico and her love of languages, and it wasn't a ploy when he interrupted her to ask.

'What are you studying now?'

'Russian.' Charlotte rolled her eyes. 'Well, when I say studying, it's just on the Internet and I *make* myself watch the Russian news… Where was I?' she asked, and he blinked, because he was having trouble remembering where he was. He was forgetting the very reason that he was here. 'I helped Nico to sort out his flight and his follow-on accommodation and he said that he needed someone part time…' She gave a tight shrug. 'I was in no position to accept his offer, of course, I spent half my life 40,000 feet in the air, but we kept in touch and now and then I'd arrange him a flight or book a hotel. But when his PA resigned I'd just left the airline…' Nothing in her voice revealed the regret in her decision, she just paused for half a second before continuing. 'It sort of grew from there.'

And something was growing here too—how, she did not know, for her guard was up and she was determined to be businesslike, but there was something about his company that engaged her, something about the hand that reached out for her as she stepped over a rock pool that steadied her stance, just not her heart.

'I ought to get back.' Charlotte reclaimed the hand that was warmed by his brief touch. 'I have to make a phone call. To my mum,' she added, because, though it didn't quite fit with her polished party-girl image, she didn't want him to think she was racing back to tell Nico. 'You can use mine.' He pulled out a slim phone from his pocket and she was about to decline, to head back to the safety of her suite, to work out what on earth she should do, but the sky was so gold and her hand was still warm from his touch, and for reasons better left unexamined she did not want their walk to end.

'It's international...' Her voice petered out along with her excuses, because the cost of a phone call would hardly be a problem to him. 'Thank you.'

Politely he walked on ahead and took a seat on a rock by the water's edge as she spent a moment locating the number and being put through.

It was heartbreaking. The confusion in her mother's voice, the pleading with Charlotte to come and save her, to bring her home, had Charlotte biting back tears as a nurse came onto the phone.

'It might be better if you don't talk to her just before

bedtime,' the nurse gently suggested. 'It unsettles her for a couple of hours after she speaks with you.'

'So it's better that she thinks I've forgotten her?' Charlotte retorted, and then apologised. "I'm sorry to snap, I just...'

'It's so hard on you.' The nurse was incredibly kind. 'If she was here permanently it would be different, but she's only with us for a few days and the change of surroundings is so unsettling, it just disorientates her all the more when you call. Why don't you ring and speak with the staff to find out how she is?'

It took a moment after hanging up to compose herself enough to join Zander, but he must have seen the glimmer of tears in her eyes because after a moment he spoke.

'You're close to your mum?'

'I don't know,' Charlotte admitted, though she had never done so before, her head still spinning from the emotion of speaking with her mother. 'I don't know if we're close or just bound...' She took a deep breath. This was not the professional conversation she was supposed to be having with him, but surely she wasn't being indiscreet in speaking about herself. Surely it was safer than speaking about Nico. And on this particular evening, knowing her mother was scared and in tears and that there was nothing she could do about it, it was easy to talk. Not that she would reveal her mother's illness to him, for she had been badly burned doing so in the past—the look of horror on her boyfriend's face when she had invited him in one night and he had witnessed the chaos that was her life, and another fledgling relationship that had ended before it had really begun when she had told him of her plight. Charlotte had long since learned where to stay quiet.

'She had me when she was older…' Charlotte said a couple of moments later, soothed by the company and the view, her ankles dangling in the water. The sky was a glorious riot of orange. She had front row seats to a show she loved, but this was surely the best one ever, the colours so vivid, the ocean so majestic. 'I think at first she wanted my dad to leave his wife…' She hadn't really told anyone this, but it was so good to talk and have someone answer. Too used to her own thoughts, it was so nice to finally share a part of herself, though she chose not to tell Zander everything, chose not to reveal all of her plight. 'She was my father's mistress. He was from London, which was why she moved there. I think she thought if she had a baby that he'd…' Charlotte gave a shrug. 'Well, it didn't work—he wanted a mistress, not a mother. He didn't leave his wife, didn't come and see us.' She gave a wry smile, for her mother had never let her forget just how much she had given up for her child. 'I always thought he'd come and live with us one day.'

'Did your mum?'

'Not in the end. By the time I was at school she'd long since given up.' Charlotte shook her head. 'She just got more bitter. I always dreamt he'd come and find us. She said that I lived with my head in the clouds…'

'Clearly you were intended to,' Zander said. 'Forty

thousand feet up in them.' And she smiled, because he had listened, really listened, and then the smile on her face faded, because she was looking at him and he was looking at her, and it was more than talking and sharing. There was more, and in that moment she knew it but forced herself to deny it, changed the conversation, for they could not sit staring endlessly, and if they did, for even a moment longer, he would kiss her. He would kiss lips that were waiting, would be accepting, but he did not move.

'What about you?' Her voice did not break the spell.

'I live with my feet on the ground,' Zander said.

'Your parents,' she asked. 'Do you still see your mother?' There was so much she wanted to know, so much Nico was desperate to find out, but, sitting there, it was not Nico she was asking Zander the questions for but herself. She wanted to know him, but it was her question that broke the moment, her words that ended the kiss that never was.

'I live in Australia,' he said, which wasn't really an answer. He turned away from her and looked out to sea, changed the subject along with the mood. 'The sunsets are spectacular here,' he said, because they were. Whatever he felt about Xanos, that much was at least true.

'The sun doesn't set,' she said. He turned again to look at her, but she did not return his gaze, just stared out into the distance. 'It's just an illusion. We're the ones moving.' Now she did turn, saw him frown and she smiled. 'It messed with my head a bit when I read it, but it's obvious really—given that the sun never moves.'

He looked back at the ocean, to another truth that was a lie, to a different way of thinking, and it messed with his head too.

'But, yes,' Charlotte said, 'it's very beautiful.'

And they sat in silence, with separate thoughts but more comfortably together. Usually when she looked to the sky she wanted to be up there, just not this evening, not this time, for now, in this moment, she was happy where she was. Then, when he stood and offered his hand, she took it, let him lead her back, and they walked ankle deep through the lapping water and she was glad to be beside him.

There was no moon and it was growing too dark for idle walking, but as they passed the beach café he did something she never thought he would. There were no fries at the upmarket beach café, but he bought two souvlakis, not for them. They stood on the beach as it grew colder and darker and fed the gulls, and she laughed like she hadn't in a very long time as the hungry, frantic birds swooped and swirled around. They headed back to the hotel and as he located discarded leather shoes and slipped them on his invitation was not unexpected. 'Let me take you to dinner.'

'I really...' She wanted to say yes to him, so badly she wanted it, but she had to speak with Nico first. It was with true regret that she declined. 'I'm actually rather tired. It's been a busy day, I might just get room service...'

He was skilled enough with women not to push.

An utter gentleman, he walked her back to the hotel foyer and even windswept and with the bottom of his trousers damp with sea water and sand, he was easily the best-dressed man there. There was an effortless elegance to him that needed neither shirt nor tie nor black credit card on show, he was easily the most beautiful. 'Nico is going to be stunned when he sees you.' Of that she was certain.

'Then tomorrow let's work out together how best to surprise him.' He saw her swallow, knew she was torn, and he moved to assure her. 'I did not want to tell him over the phone. I want to see his face when he realises we have found each other. Perhaps tomorrow you will say yes to joining me for dinner?'

The bar was in full swing; beautiful couples and stunning singles were everywhere, and a piano was playing a gentle invitation. He saw her eyes drift towards it, knew he could perhaps secure a drink, and then dinner, and then who knew? But he was far cleverer than that and now they were back in the hotel she was as wary as a kitten.

He took her hand and Charlotte jumped at the contact then shivered as he did the most old-fashioned thing: he picked it up and held her fingers to his lips and briefly kissed her hand.

It looked formal, it felt anything but. The weight of soft lips on her hand made her stomach curl, had her thoughts skittering, her world confused, for she had never had such an intense response to a man, to any man.

It had been a great relief in fact that, despite her boss's devastating good looks, he did absolutely nothing for her, or Charlotte for him. Even prior to his wedding there had been nothing, not a hint of flirting, yet here stood a man in Nico's image, and she wanted to sink to her knees. Everything around this man made her feel weak and confused. His black eyes lifted to her burning face, his lips dropped contact, but she could feel the warmth of them still on her skin and if he were to ask her for dinner again, she could only say yes.

'Enjoy the rest of your evening.'

He bade her goodnight, saw the battle between relief and disappointment flare in her eyes and how delicious it would be tomorrow, he consoled himself, how much sweeter for waiting.

Would she tell Nico?

He watched her walk away and could not quite decide, but he had done his best to prevent it, bar tying her to a bed...

His tongue rolled in his cheek at the very thought, moved to his lips, tasting where her flesh had been, and he resisted the urge to follow, to ask her again, for never did Zander ask twice; instead, he headed to the bar.

She walked across the foyer, willed herself not to turn around, but want was stronger and as she made it to the lifts she allowed herself one tiny peek, hoped against hope that he was walking behind her, that Zander would ask her again, or at least be heading to his room, but, no, he was heading to the bar. She saw the unaccompanied females perk up as he stepped in. He said something to a waiter and then briefly turned around and caught her looking.

God, but she wanted to run to him. To go to the bar and claim her prize.

It was safer, though, to be away from him.

She made it to her room and closed the door, even slid the security chain, not to keep him out but more to keep her in.

Away from him she could think, could take a shower and slip into a robe, could order room service and remember who was her boss.

Loyalty was everything to Charlotte and without the flexibility of this job she shuddered to think what she would do. She had to ring him, had to tell him what she now knew, and away from the intensity of Zander, normality was returning.

'Nico…' She bit back a hiss of frustration at the sound of his voicemail. 'It's Charlotte—I'm in Xanos and something rather unexpected has come up. Could you call me back, please?'

He did not.

Again, as the maids came for turn-down service, she tried her boss's number, sat on the balcony, huddled in her dressing gown, cold but grateful for it, watching the delicious water. She got Nico's voicemail again, turning in surprise when a maid came out and served her a small glass of Raki and bade her goodnight. She took a sip, grimacing at the taste but liking the burn and hoping it would help her rest. Hope was short-lived for glancing above she looked straight into the eyes of Zander. He stood, glass in hand, on a vast balcony at the top. His eyes homed in on her and she sat there, frozen, like a mouse beneath a hawk and she thought he might swoop down and claim her.

She retreated to her room, slid the glass door closed and dropped the catch, scared not of Zander but of herself, of the woman inside who was screaming to be let out.

'Nico, please…' She rang again, just before she headed to bed. She slept with her phone beside her and when it rang at seven, she willed it to be her boss, but the devil inside leapt with delight when she heard Zander's voice.

'How about breakfast?'

She moved to the window, peered out, and could see him on his balcony, just a towel around his waist.

'I'm not sure.' She was hesitant, not just because of what Nico might say, more because this was a man no woman could safely handle. Even from this distance his beauty was evident.

'On the beach,' he added, and still she did not respond. 'I will have them pack a hamper. It's up to you if you join me. I'll be there in half an hour.'

CHAPTER THREE

ZANDER walked along the golden beach of Xanos, but as scenic as the view was, as pleasant the water, his stomach churned with bile. Everywhere his gaze fell brought a fresh memory, spearing his scalp as if arrows were aimed at it.

Why had he bought the south of the island? Why had he invested so much time and money in a place he would rather forget?

He should have left well alone.

He looked towards the land, to the vast complex he had built, and he thought of the scaled model that was in his office in Australia. Usually he was hands on with his investments, but not this time. He had vowed never to return, yet here he was, and no matter how accurate the model, it was different seeing the real thing—seeing firsthand the houses that would soon be bulldozed to make way for a nightclub and more shops and restaurants. He looked to where Nico lived and knew it had once been their grandfather's home, that their mother had been raised there. How it hurt to be back on Xanos sand. Yes, it had been a magnificent investment. Perhaps only a local could ever have envisaged the true potential of the hidden side of Xanos—the humble fishing village that was just waiting to be transformed—yet for all the prestige and profit, for all the erasure of the landscape he hated, all this place had ever brought him was pain, and it was doing so now.

His head throbbed from lack of sleep and he turned his mind to tomorrow, to the long-awaited confrontation with his twin—and Zander wondered if he had blown it, for no doubt Charlotte would have rung her boss already. He should have stayed in his suite, should have spent the weekend in isolation. Yet, Zander mused as he walked, he had enjoyed spending time with Charlotte. He glanced up at the hotel. Used to staring at the model in his office, he easily worked out which was her room, thought of her in it and wondered if she was preparing to join him.

It had not been his intention to call her this morning, but he had thought of the day that stretched ahead, the wait that that would be interminable without diversion.

'Forget it,' he told himself, heading back to his suite, and to the shower. He would contact her later, take her to dinner—women were for the night-time, a reward for hard work, a balm for insomnia, not for spending the day with. Still, he was curious whether she had told Nico, which, he told himself, was the reason he had called her.

Charlotte approached, and she was nervous, dressed in shorts and a strappy vest, topped with the previous day's cardigan. Her eyes were bruised with lack of sleep

courtesy of this very man. Another call to Nico had gone
unanswered and, as gorgeous as the smile was as Zander
turned to greet her, still she would set the ground rules.

'Morning.' She made herself say it. 'I'd prefer not to
speak about Nico.'

'Of course not,' Zander said.

'I just don't feel comfortable…' She was honest with
this. 'I haven't been able to contact him yet.'

'You don't have to explain yourself. I'm just glad that
you joined me. Let's see what they have prepared.'

The hotel had put on a sumptuous breakfast and they
sat on the deserted beach and she drank hot chocolate,
while Zander chose coffee. They both ate yoghurt driz-
zled with passion fruit and then pastries, which Zander
thought tasted somehow sweeter this morning.

'I love seeing new places.' Charlotte dug her toes
into the sand, looked up at the sky and to the flash of a
silver plane but again, with him beside her, she did not
want to be up there.

'What do you miss most about travelling?' He followed her gaze.

'All of it really.' She gave a smile. 'Except the un-
packing. I don't know, I love airports, the excitement.
I love going to new places, exploring them. My friend
Shirley and I…' She did not continue, for sometimes she
choked a little when she thought of those times, and the
hours between flights that had been spent so well.

'Have you looked around Xanos?'

'Not yet,' Charlotte said. 'Maybe later today.' He
was such good company, such an intriguing man, be-

cause it was not he who pushed for information. Instead, Charlotte asked the questions for he fascinated her so. When asked, he told her about his hotel chain, about the casinos he owned, about his life on the other side of the world.

'You must have missed this, though,' Charlotte offered, turning to watch as he stared out to the Mediterranean, just as he had yesterday.

'Australia is hardly lacking in beaches,' Zander pointed out. 'I have an office and a property in Sydney that overlooks what is arguably the most beautiful harbour in the world.' If it sounded like a boast, it had not been intended as one. More, Zander was trying to convince himself. For how could he miss a place that had brought nothing but pain—a view, this view, that as a child and later as a teenager he had wept into.

It should be hard to fathom now, strong, independent, beyond wealthy, it should be impossible to recall with precision just how afraid and confused he had once been, but when he looked out to the ocean, to a small mound of rocks a few hundred metres out where the waves crashed and broke up, he could wipe away twenty years. He could feel the fear and the confusion, the bruises on his back and legs from his father's beating, the wrenching pain that came with true hunger and the bewilderment of being left behind—that a mother, his mother, might have left him to deal with this. It was painful to recall it even now.

Each minute that passed brought him a minute closer to his brother, to the twin his mother had chosen to take.

Each minute that passed brought him closer to the confrontation of which he had long dreamed, the moment where he would finally face the brother who had lived in the lap of luxury while he had eaten from bins, the brother who had had been given the velvet-glove treatment, while he had been ruled by a fist.

'Every beach is different though…' Charlotte's voice was softer than his thoughts. 'And this feels like a slice of heaven.'

Or hell.

'It was not all happy.' He heard his voice, heard his own words, and it stunned him into silence, for he never revealed anything and certainly he should not to the PA of his twin. And yet as she turned, as she did not speak, just moved her mouth into a wry smile, she offered not words but the space of her mind. She turned her attention fully to him, and for once he did not want to retreat. 'The memories are not all good.'

'But are there some good ones?'

And his mind shifted because, yes, there had been some. He looked back at the ocean, to the same mound of rocks, and recalled teenage boys jumping, he in the middle, egging each other on. He remembered waiting for the tourist buses before it had turned more sordid, when pretty young things would arrive and he could escape. He remembered then the happier bits, instead of later—when he had relied on his looks to secure a bed, had kissed older, drunk women, for it had meant breakfast the next day. And his mind turned to the market at the north of the island, to being chased for stealing fruit and then laughing with friends as they'd eaten. There had been no innocence in his youth, but there had been some fun.

'We would go to the market...' Again, he was stunned that he told her, yet it felt good to speak, to share with another. 'We were about twelve.' He told her of the thieving and she laughed, but not too much, for after all he had been hungry. And he told her too of the taverna that would fill with tourists at night, how he had always looked older... He did not tell her about the women, or scrabbling through the bins out the back for something to eat. He told her the better bits and smiled at the better bits, and then Zander surprised himself again.

'I will show you Xanos,' he offered. 'The real Xanos.'

She thought, because it was Zander, that she would be swallowed again by a huge limo, that the island of Xanos would be revealed to her through thick darkened glass, but instead he rang ahead and by the time they had made their way back, to her surprise and nervous delight two scooters had been delivered to the foyer of the hotel.

'I've never ridden a scooter...'

'I thought you liked exploring.'

'On foot,' Charlotte said, and then laughed. 'Or on camel.'

He smiled at the thought. 'Few tourists have ridden a scooter when they come here. You'll soon pick it up.'

She wanted him to change his mind, to offer to let her climb on his scooter, to coast the island nestled into his back, but never did he offer easy; instead, he pushed her out of her comfort zone. She was grateful for it, for after a few nervous goes she enjoyed the thrill of riding her little scooter, the absence of a helmet not the only rule that was broken. With Zander she felt as if she were flying the trapeze without a safety net. It was wild and dangerous, the thrill of the chase, cat and mouse, as he accelerated ahead of her and waited for her to catch up, then sped off, laughing again.

The only blot on her happiness was a phone that still had not rung, and as they parked their bikes in the marketplace and they walked into a taverna, she caught him looking as she checked her phone.

'It's up to you whether or not you tell him, Charlotte,' Zander said as they took a seat. 'I don't want to put pressure on you. I just had hoped to surprise him. I have long thought of the day that we see each other again.'

'He's my boss,' she attempted, and thankfully he did seem to understand.

'I have put you in an impossible situation,' Zander said. 'Really, I should have just stayed in my suite. I should be there now...' He looked into her eyes and the world seemed to stop. 'But then we would have missed out on our day, so I cannot regret it.'

Neither could she.

It seemed like for ever since she had been so self-indulgent, not just with the food or the views, but with the company and conversation, and though she did her utmost to remain distant, warned herself it was a distinct lack of male company in recent years that made Zander impress her so—that a couple of years ago, she could so easily have handled him—she knew that she was lying to herself. For in whatever life she might be living, in whatever circumstances they might meet, Zander would have consumed her on sight.

'Soon you will be back in London,' Zander said, 'and I will be back in Australia.' His words were a brutal reminder that all they had was measured in days, a warning—or was it permission he was giving her?— to just enjoy this, to be the glamorous party girl that he perceived she was. 'To our day,' he said, and raised his glass. How delicious the sparkling water tasted as it slid down her throat, how heady and exhilarating it was to be with him, but she felt her face redden when her phone rang. There was sweat beading on her lip, which probably wasn't the most attractive of looks, but she was not thinking of that as she picked up her phone and saw that finally Nico was returning her call.

'Excuse me a moment.' Charlotte stood. 'I might take this outside.'

He wanted to know what was discussed, he *needed* to know, so Zander had a word with the waiter and handed him a very nice tip, warning him to be discreet. The waiter then headed out to clear the tables.

Charlotte took a seat at a small table, and took a deep breath as she answered, nervous to tell Nico but knowing she had to, no matter what Zander might think, no matter the surprise she spoiled, Nico was her boss and somehow, despite the dizzying effect of Zander close by, she must keep her head and remember that fact.

'Charlotte, it's Constantine.' The sound of Nico's wife

caught her by surprise. 'Nico knows you've been trying to get hold of him—he asked me to ring you back.'

'I really need to speak with him.'

'His father's been taken ill,' Constantine explained, and then clarified. 'His adoptive father. You know things have been tense…' Charlotte was quiet as Constantine took a steadying breath. Tense was the understatement of the year, for since Nico had guessed that he had been adopted, the already fragile relationship with his father had been tested beyond its limits. His adoptive parents had not even attended the wedding, and Charlotte closed her eyes in sympathy as Constantine made things frighteningly clear. 'He's on the small hospital in Lathira, but Nico is having him flown now to the mainland as things are very serious. Nico will be at the meeting tomorrow, but for now he asks that you hold the fort. He wants you to arrange a seven a.m. flight from Athens—he really wants to attend the meeting—but then he will fly directly back.'

'The thing is…' Charlotte attempted, but she halted. She could hear the chimes of the hospital, their baby, Leo, was crying too, and now was not the time. How could she reveal something so personal, and not even to Nico himself? Perhaps Zander was right. The surprise would be more meaningful coming from his brother and surely Nico did not need any extra stress right now. 'Tell Nico everything is fine. Tell him that there is good news waiting for him when he gets to Xanos and give him my best wishes.'

'I will. I have to go now, Charlotte.'

She rang off the phone and sat silent for a moment, declined when a nice waiter offered to bring her drink outside. 'It's okay—I'll be back in a moment.'

So she was on her own with the secret.

She looked into the bar where Zander sat and, to his credit, he did not look over, was not trying to work out what she had said to his brother and to see if she had spoiled the surprise; instead, he chatted to the waiter as his glass was refilled and smiled as she walked back into the taverna.

'Do you want to eat lunch here?' She was incredibly grateful that he did not try to delve, did not ask what she had said to Nico, and she returned his smile, with one that came from the bottom of heart, for now she trusted him.

'That would be lovely.'

She trusted this beautiful man to do the right thing by her boss, and by her.

Believed in tomorrow as she sat down and Zander took her hand.

After all, she had no reason to think otherwise.

He ordered hot peppered calamari and for Zander it was good to be back, to sit at a table with money in his wallet, to look the owner in the eye when he came in and laugh as he called out something in Greek.

'What did he say?' Charlotte asked, wishing her Greek was better.

'"Alexandros, you were banned from here,"' Zander translated, and then she was treated to that stunning smile. 'Then he said, "Welcome back".'

'Alexandros?'

'As I was then.' He looked into eyes that were blue, eyes that held his, eyes that made him go on. 'After my father.'

'He's…' Charlotte swallowed, for this much Nico had told her. 'He's deceased?'

'He is.'

'And your mother?'

And the question that yesterday had been probing felt different now, more like natural conversation, but if he answered with truth, if she glimpsed his hate, she'd be gone. All Zander knew was that he did not want that, he wanted this day, so his answer was guarded instead. 'I've never known my mother.'

'Did you always know that you had a twin?'

'I thought Nico was off limits,' Zander said. 'Your rule.' He gave her a smile as he stood and put down some money for the bill. 'Come on, we can ride to the hills.'

It was a day that was, for both of them, different.

For later, as afternoon turned to evening, as they parked the scooters and walked high in the hills of Xanos, the air chilly now, he was not plotting revenge, or thinking about tomorrow. Instead, he was thinking beyond that to a place he had never been—could almost see her in his world.

'I have hotels and casinos across Australasia. I do a lot of travelling…' They stopped at a flat rock and she nodded when he suggested that they take a moment to relax. She sat on the rock, enjoying the view, not just of

Xanos but of a world he was painting for her. 'You've been to Singapore?'

'Not on my route.' Charlotte smiled.

'Then you have missed an amazing place. There is good shopping, amazing salons...' She gave a wry smile, for dressed in her work best, with her finger- and toenails painted and her roots freshly done, her eyebrows newly shaped, it was a natural assumption that this was how she lived. Despite the coolness, her cheeks reddened, for all the lies she had told, the weddings and cocktails and long lunches with friends that had never happened. 'Unlike your boss, I would want my PA to be around...' He saw a blush darken her cheeks as he gently explored what was becoming an option. A job that was a hundred per cent glamour. He could give her this every day, instead of it being a rare treat.

'I thought we weren't talking about Nico.'

'We're not,' Zander said, 'we're talking about work.'

'I'm very happy with what I do now.' She stood as if to catch her breath, but instead it was to bite down on a sudden urge to weep, for he was offering her the world, and how she wanted to say yes, to be the woman he thought she was—if only she could be.

'I would pay you more.' He wanted his way, he always got his way, and he would have it now.

'It's not about money!' Her voice came out shrill, too sharp, too strained to pretend she was not upset. She could barely manage to keep up the façade for a week, let alone permanently.

'I would look after you better than he,' Zander said,

and he meant it. For he *would* look after her and that would start now.

Zander *was* at his most potent. The walk in the hills that had seemingly so naturally unfolded had been absolutely contrived. This was a route he had trodden so many times in his youth. It was no convenient rock they had ambled towards—this was his stomping ground, here, where with women he had always got his way. The letters 'AK' were carved in the rock beneath the moss where her bottom had sat.

'Zander, I don't know if I've…' How could she say it, how could she tell him about her real and drab life? She had not set out to lie, but knew of course that she had. 'I think I've misled you…' She saw his face darken. And darken it did as he braced himself to hear that Nico was, as he surely had already known, far more than a boss. 'I haven't told you—'

'Don't,' he interrupted her, for he did not need to hear it. He did not need an angel, Zander reminded himself, he was here only to get revenge. 'You don't have to say anything.' And then he said something else, something that, despite the cool Xanos breeze, made her warm inside, had her sit back down when his hand took her wrist. 'Let us enjoy *our* day.' She wanted that, wanted so very much this escape. She did not want to cloud it, to spoil it, to bring reality in to this magical place. 'Maybe you'll think about my job offer later, maybe…'

'I…' How could she say that she wouldn't think about it when it was all she would ever think about, even if it could never be? She closed her eyes and entered the luxury of his offer, working for him, seeing more of him, and then as his lips dusted her mouth, they confirmed the full extent of the debauchery behind his proposition. Yet it did not offend, it was the most delicious sensation she had felt in years, his lips warmer than her cool ones, his mouth so much more in control than hers. All she did was feel it—feel the warm pulse of his flesh on hers. She relished the weight of a mouth that moved slowly, a mouth that warmed rapidly, and she took his breath into her and held it, and held it some more, and then breathed it back to him and now they were one. It was one kiss that both were sharing, for now her mouth moved on his, now she tasted him, and their kiss was a slow one, a warning, a heady warning that there was so much more to come.

When Zander kissed, it was always with intent, a means to an end, a temporary place where he'd prefer not to linger, and now, in a minute, his hand would wander. Soon, in a minute, he would press her back to lie on the mossy stone, but there were things in this kiss that he had never noticed before, that her eyelashes swept on his temple and that the tip of her tongue was like a balm that made him forget the hell.

Sex made him forget, he reminded himself, kissing her just a little bit harder, for surely that was where this must lead, but she seemed to want more of a taste of him and, yes, he actually liked her tongue's tentative exploration, liked the faint taste of their breaths mingled. Had it not been so delicious he would have taken her right there on the hillside, would have moved his hand from

A to B and then a moment later a little lower again—
would have worked the trusted formula that never failed.
Had their kiss not been so unusually pleasing, he would
have had her panties in his hand just about now, except
all they were doing were kissing, and he did not want
Charlotte bare-bottomed on a hill.

Oh, but he did, Zander thought as his mouth still
moved hers and his ardor deepened as, not on formula
but instinct, his hand moved beneath her waist to the
low rise of her shorts. He wanted his fingers to slip in
there, wanted where this could so, so easily lead, but he
did not want her embarrassment afterwards. He resisted
the lure of her zip and his fingers moved to the hemline,
dug into her tender inner thigh as he attempted a rapid
halt but it was she kissing him now, her tongue calling
the shots.

She hadn't been kissed in so very long, and never
more thoroughly than now—so expert his tongue, so
blissful his hands, so faint-making his scent, all she
wanted was to give in to the press of his mouth and
move backwards, to lie down under him, to relish the
bliss of his hands—hands that slid from her arm to her
waist. There was the faint brush of his thumb on her
nipple and the sound of foreign birdsong, and so easily
he took her away, so tenderly he removed each splin-
ter on her mind, each shackle to her heart that with one
kiss she forgot what she knew. With his kiss she lost the
hurt and forgot to be wary.

His hands were near her bottom and then moving
around to the front, the weight of him pinning her down,

then the bliss of his fingers pressing into her thighs, climbing and then resting and then slowly climbing again as her mouth beckoned him on and, with his kiss, it was hard to remember she was here to work, here as Nico's PA. Somehow, as his mouth dragged her under, as his kisses pressed her down to the mossy rock beneath, her mind fought its way to the surface, resisted delicious temptation and remembered the reason she was here.

'Nico!' He heard the word in his mouth and he almost spat it out, heard her say his twin's name as he kissed her, and as her head pulled back, so too did his.

'The name's Zander!' Black were the eyes that looked down at her, and the tone of his voice sent a chill through her.

'I meant…' Did he really think she had mistaken him, that in the throes of passion she had been thinking of Nico? 'I forgot that I'm supposed to be at work.' Surely she must have mistaken the ice in his voice and the anger in his eyes, for there was no trace of either now, just the familiar smile that warmed and a brief kiss to her lips as still he pressed on top of her that told her all was okay. 'I don't think I should be here.'

He actually agreed, for the mossy hillside was not where he wanted to sample Charlotte. He wanted her only in his bed now. He wanted her writhing and sobbing beneath him, wanted to ensure a future where it was *his* name she sobbed into Nico's mouth.

'Look.' She aimed for confidence in her voice, even

if she could not quite meet his eyes. 'That should never have happened…'

'That?' Zander said, and his fingers gently stroked, crept up, just a little, but enough to remind her where they'd been heading. 'Or this?' He was still lying over her; she could feel his erection pressed into her hip, could feel his fingers at the hem of her shorts, and she felt as if the devil was beckoning.

It would be so much easier to simply kiss that mouth back, to deliciously resume; but the ease of her response to him unnerved her—and not for a moment could he comprehend how out of character this was, that the polished, sophisticated, well-travelled woman was, in fact, a ghost from her past, not the Charlotte she had now become. Neither would he understand that even the Charlotte of old would never have found herself half-naked on a hillside, that only with him had this wanton woman emerged.

'None of it,' she attempted, except it died on her lips, because back in London her only regret would surely be halting things.

'Well, for what it's worth…' he kissed her cheek as he released her '…I'm glad that it did. Let's get you back.' It was Zander, slightly breathless as he stood, Zander who rearranged her clothes and then offered his hand. As she took it, she felt as if she was handing over her heart, felt for a giddy moment as if she'd found the one person who would take care of her. Damp night swirled in on Xanos, and her head was literally in the clouds as she walked down the hillside with him.

'What is that bird?' She could hear the same call that had danced in her mind as he had kissed her, its song following her now down the hillside and she craned her neck, her eyes scanning the trees to glimpse the bird that made the strange '*po-po*' call.

'It's the hoopoe bird,' Zander explained. 'You rarely see them, you just hear them, but they are beautiful birds. They'll be gone soon…'

Like you, Charlotte thought as they walked down the hillside, a rare beauty she had briefly glimpsed but could never hope to truly capture. She wanted to be back in his arms, wanted more of his kiss, but instead she held onto his hand as they walked and Zander talked.

'They head to the Canary Islands for the colder months.'

'It's a strange call.' She stood for a moment and listened, drank in the unfamiliar sound, wanted to remember the Xanos hillside for ever. 'So relaxing.'

'Not for the locals.' Zander interrupted her thoughts. 'They say when the hoopoe sings in the evening then soon there will be war. It's just superstition.' He smiled as her eyes widened. 'The island is full of it.' His hand was warm around hers, his smile reassuring. 'You like birds?'

'I guess,' Charlotte said as they reached their scooters. 'I think I like anything that can fly.'

They rode back to the hotel, and only as she climbed off the scooter in such gorgeous surroundings did she realise how grubby and unkempt the day had made her, but she felt as if she was wearing a ballgown as he offered his arm and they walked inside.

'We will meet for dinner,' Zander said, for he would not take no tonight. 'I'll call for you in an hour. What is your room number?' He was so direct, so all-assuming. Again she reminded herself that Nico was her boss. She had to somehow wrestle control back, for around Zander she had virtually none.

'I haven't said yes yet.'

Oh, you just did, Zander thought, for he could see her pulse leaping above her collarbone, could almost smell the want that was in the air.

'Fine,' Zander said, and as he had last night he made as if to leave it, even turned his back and went to walk away, so positive was he she would call him back, but he was caught off guard by her words.

'Perhaps I should offer to take you to dinner,' Charlotte said, and he turned his head. 'I am sure Nico would expect no less.'

She saw his eyes shutter, for a moment thought she might have offended him, but when she looked again he was smiling, and she must have imagined the flash of darkness.

'I'll meet you in the foyer,' Charlotte said, not sure she wanted this stunning man knocking at her hotel-room door, not sure at all that she could resist him.

'I'll look forward to it' was all that Zander said.

And so too would she.

She rang the nursing home and, as advised, spoke not to her mother but to the staff and was informed that

Amanda had settled in a little better, which should have reassured her, but she didn't quite believe it was true.

'If she does get upset,' Charlotte said, 'please remind her that this is just temporary, that I'll be home in a couple of days.'

It might bring comfort to Amanda, but it brought little to Charlotte. She truly didn't know if she missed her mum, if she even wanted to get back to her real life. There was guilt with the realisation, guilt that seemed to layer on guilt, but she quashed it. She was determined to just enjoy her time her on Xanos, to go back a better daughter for the temporary reprieve.

He was a reprieve, Charlotte told herself, a brief indulgence that she could handle, dinner and perhaps one more kiss.

As she undressed in the bathroom, slipped her freshly foiled hair into a hotel shower cap, she felt more like the old Charlotte than she ever had—felt like the jet-set woman she once had been, a woman who could handle a man like Zander Kargas.

It was bliss to sink into the bath, and more to step out of the bathroom and to see the pulled curtains, to resist the temptation to open them. It was heady and dizzy but she felt as if his eyes could burn through the fabric as she massaged her skin with oil, felt as if he was watching her as she dressed slowly.

For him.

Somehow he made the fantasy real.

Made her feel special enough to take that extra care.

She was used to doing her hair quickly, so she stood

in the marble bathroom and smoothed it out with her trusty straighteners, but it needed something more so she skilfully spun thick, heavy ringlets, over and over again, each one, Charlotte thought, for Zander. With each curl, she imagined his fingers through it later, and then told herself there could be none of that.

She told herself he was a guest of Nico's tonight, if only to help herself behave.

There wasn't really much decision as to what to wear. She had brought her faithful travel wardrobe of old, which consisted of a black evening dress, a touch slinky with spaghetti straps, and a small wrap, or another more demure dress, a soft brushed velvet in chocolate brown with a cowl neck.

She settled for the brown.

Hoped the demure cut of the dress might calm her but, even slipping it on, the sex in her mind brought the dress to life; the fabric seemed tighter around her bust and more clingy over her hips. Her eyes glittered in anticipation and her cheeks glowed at the very thought of Zander. She begged herself to reel it in. She had to keep her head for one night, one night only, for tomorrow the secret would be out. Tomorrow she could fall into his arms, as she now so badly wanted to.

She was dizzy with lust as she sprayed fragrance not just on her wrists and neck but the backs of her knees too. She imagined his mouth there on the tender flesh and she knew she must not, that tonight somehow she had to resist him, that tomorrow, after tomorrow, when he and Nico were reconciled, when things were more ordered, then she could think about them.

Except she could only think about him.

Could only shiver at the memory of his kiss.

It wasn't a date. It was *not* a date, she told herself, but it felt like it was as she glossed her lips and had one final check in the mirror.

Zander was absolutely potent and she had to keep her head tonight, had to see how things went with Nico and Zander before she did anything. She almost doubled up then, stunned at the possibilities her mind lurched to, for he made her feel rash, dizzy, to *want*.

Zander too smiled as he looked into the mirror.

Tonight would be such an unexpected treat.

He had enjoyed flirting with Charlotte on the phone, getting her to open up a little, and though last night he had more intended to loosen her tongue with fine wine, the stakes were raised now. He had not anticipated the rare beauty of her, that she might live up to the voice he had enjoyed these past weeks.

Now he wanted her.

Wanted her to sob *his* name into his brother's mouth. How sweet was delayed revenge, for he wanted everything his brother had and then some more, but the thought of her with another made him churn in a way he never had before. As he stared into the mirror he chose not to shave, just splashed on cologne. Then his thoughts were darker, his intent deeper, for he would leave Nico with nothing, as he had been left with nothing, and his mind was made up. It was not a cruel decision, Zander told himself as he headed down to meet her. He might be misleading her but soon she would come to understand.

Tonight he would have Charlotte in his bed.

Tomorrow she would be in his life.

CHAPTER FOUR

CHARLOTTE had worked long enough with Nico to know how he liked things, and what he expected from her when dealing with clients. She knew as she arrived before their arranged time that, despite the butterflies in her stomach, despite the thrill of an evening with Zander, she was, even if Nico was unaware, working for her boss tonight.

She did as Nico would expect of her—arriving in the foyer a full fifteen minutes early, she whiled the time away till Zander arrived looking into the boutique windows at the bags and purses with leather so soft they seemed to beg her to go in and stroke them. She wandered to the jeweller's, blinked at the most stunning of necklaces, thick with rubies and diamonds. She had possibly never seen anything so lovely.

'It would look good around your neck.'

She heard his words, heard his greeting, smelt the freshly washed male scent of him. It felt as if not the necklace but Zander was around her throat, for it was so tight as she turned to greet him.

Oh, he had once looked like Nico, but now, to

Charlotte, all he was was Zander. There could be no mistake ever again. It wasn't just that Zander's hair was a little longer, his strong jaw shadowed, his eyelids slightly heavier lidded, his skin a touch darker. With Zander she felt far from safe, for each parting meant a new greeting and each time the stakes seemed raised. She registered the flare of danger that ignited whenever he approached, acknowledged that he took her, without asking, completely out of her usual bounds. It was Sunday night in Xanos, the dress code smart casual, and Zander wore it incredibly well—black dinner trousers with a white fitted shirt that showed his toned body. His hair was tousled but gleaming yet there was an edge to him, something in the unshaven jaw and black gypsy eyes that set him apart, a statement made without words, something that warned he had never been and could never be tamed.

'Have you been waiting long?' Zander asked.

'Not at all,' she tried, even if it was a little late to do so, to sound professional, to make things clear, to draw a safe line. 'Anyway, you're my guest.'

'Had you been mine,' Zander pointed out as the *maître d'* suggested they take a seat at the bar and their table would be ready in a few moments, 'our table would have already been ready.'

Not used to waiting, especially in a hotel he owned, Zander did not actually mind, for instead of the clean white linen and neat order of the restaurant they were led to a dark sultry bar that was to be their holding pen. He had seen the designs, the finished product on the computer, had even been in here last night, but had not really appreciated it till now.

Zander suppressed a smile as she sat down, her bottom lower than her knees on the extremely low couches, revealing a stretch of thigh. It was not his fault, of course, that he sat just an inch too close, that the soft plush of the sofa rolled his body in just a little, till the fabric of his black trousers almost melted as it encountered her flesh. He felt her attempt a discreet wriggle away as she tried not to touch him, but there was nowhere to go.

'I'm sorry about this.' She tried a smile that was supposed to come out professional and businesslike, tried to pretend that it was Nico for whom the table was not waiting, because with him she could talk, could laugh and yet reveal nothing. 'The table shouldn't be much longer.'

'I'm more than happy to wait,' Zander said as their drinks were delivered.

As she sat too close to this dangerous image, this sexy version of her boss, Charlotte felt as if she was in some erotic dream, some wild, vivid dream, where she would be unable to look at Nico in the morning thinking of the terrible, reckless, depraved things she had done with his twin, for how could a mouth look so divine just biting into the lime of his gin? How could a finger look so sexy and dark and debauched as it stirred the ice though his drink?

There was no lack of manners, he was not being rude,

but it was sex and she knew it. He melted the ice with his finger as he was melting her now.

'Where were we?' Zander said, and she struggled to remember whatever it was she'd been saying, struggled to keep her head in the most oppressive environments.

'About to have dinner,' Charlotte said, her eyes pleading for the waiter, for the summons to their table, for she could feel the length of his thigh against hers, remembered the press of him on the Xanos hillside. She had been a fool to think she could handle this, that for a moment she could resist the potent force of him.

'And how was your day?'

'Fine.' It was she being the rude one. 'Pleasant, in fact.'

'We could eat here,' he offered, and her eyes darted from him to the bar. Sure enough, people were eating at the tables. 'Shall I suggest…?'

Thank God for the waiter who came and told them their table was ready. She almost wept with relief as she stood, pulled down her dress over her thighs, tried to rearrange not just her clothes but her mind into some semblance of decency as they walked though the restaurant to a beautifully laid table. The music in the background was so unobtrusive she was sure the entire room must be able to hear her heart.

The waiter informed them that it was too cool and windy tonight for the balcony table she had ordered, which was a regret for her cheeks were on fire.

'I didn't order champagne,' Zander said as they were seated and the waiter started to pour it.

'I did.' She sat and gave him a smile. 'If he was aware of who my guest was tonight, Nico would insist. Anyway, I thought it appropriate, given that tomorrow you finally meet.'

He wanted to be wining and dining Charlotte; he did not want to sit here with his brother's PA, drinking champagne his brother would pay for, eating food that he had bought. He wanted nothing from Nico—well, no charity anyway. He wanted to take from him rather than receive, but not by a flicker did he betray the dark thoughts. Instead, he turned his charm to high beam, knew he could not be resisted. In the glare at first she attempted to resist, but he watched her melt, watched her weaken, and he would have her tonight, Zander decided. She would walk into the meeting tomorrow with the bruises from his mouth on her neck. Better, Zander decided, when he had told his brother his feelings, he would leave the meeting with her, would take Charlotte as his.

His for a while, Zander thought, because that was all it ever was.

The menu had delicious offerings and, grateful for reprieve from his gaze, Charlotte pored over it. It was a mixture of traditional Greek with a contemporary twist.

'I'd like the dips.'

'We are in Xanos,' Zander said. 'Why not try the crab ravioli? There is none finer.'

'I'd like the dips,' Charlotte said, but she chose fish for her main and winced just a little as he ordered herbed milk-fed lamb. 'Are you looking forward to tomorrow?'

'I'm not thinking about tomorrow.' Zander replied. 'Instead, I am enjoying tonight.'

'But…' She tried to quash her frustration. Almost every conversation was off limits till he met with her boss, yet there was so much she wanted to know about him, so much she wanted to share with him.

'I'd far rather hear about you,' Zander said.

Except that was off limits too. She didn't want the fantasy to end with the drudgery of her real life served up at this sumptuous dinner table, didn't want to watch his black eyes glaze as she droned on about her problems.

'It's a beautiful hotel…' she said.

'You'd have seen a few in your travels,' Zander commented. 'But, yes, it is.' He looked over at her. 'Have you tried the spa?'

'I'm here to work,' Charlotte said, for she was conscientious, and though she had had more than a peek at the luxurious spa menu, she would never expect Nico to foot such a bill.

'I am very proud of it,' Zander said. 'With all my hotels, I try for something different yet somehow the same.'

Their starters were delivered. She took one look at his ravioli and, though the dips were the best she'd tasted, she couldn't help but wish she'd taken his advice.

'Here.' He cut off a large piece and she thought he would place it on her plate but it was Zander, so of course the fork, *his* fork, went straight towards her mouth. She opened a jaw that felt rigid, tried to tell herself to relax, to take the offering, but with him it was so loaded. She tasted the butter on her tongue and tried to remember to swallow, tried not to ponder how with Zander everything tasted of sex.

'Tastes good, yes?'

She nodded. It was all she could manage. She licked a trickle of butter that was on her lip and as she did so the smile he gave her told her their minds were thinking along the same lines. He watched her toying with her food and, rather than summon the waiter, he moved forward a little to pour her more wine, which gave him the excuse to press his knee in. To his satisfaction she leaped as if branded, and then put a hand over her glass too late, for the champagne met slender fingers and bubbled and fizzed.

He took her hand and wanted to suck each finger dry. Perhaps, from the tremble that shot through her body, he could have got away with it, but she thought him a gentleman, and for now he obliged, took a thick white napkin and wrapped it around her hand.

And not a drop more passed her lips, and though somehow she made it through the main course, the conversation was awkward. He knew she was on guard, knew she was wrestling, could feel her nerves as the dessert menu was presented, as the evening neared a close.

'I'm not sure if I'm hungry.' She wasn't hungry, but surely it was better to be here in the restaurant than saying goodnight, trying to resist his kiss. If he did kiss her again, which he would, she knew exactly where it might lead, so she stared at the dessert menu till it blurred out of focus.

'If you're having trouble choosing, we can get a couple,' Zander offered. 'We can *share*.'

'It's terribly warm,' Charlotte said. She was babbling a little, Zander realised. 'I won't be a moment.'

He did not want to be here, fed by his brother. He wanted Charlotte for himself, on his terms.

He walked and found her easily, tucked away on the balcony, staring out to the Mediterranean, the wind blowing her curls around her face, and he could see from her profile she was troubled.

She knew he was approaching and was scared to turn around in case she fell against him.

So hard she wrestled with her conscience as she stood there.

She did not fall into bed with men. There had been a couple of relationships—one that had ended almost as soon as it had begun when she had told him about her mother's illness and one that had meant a lot but had faded and died as her mother's illness had become more and more consuming, but it was Zander consuming her now.

Zander was the first man in ages she had responded to, the first man she had ever reacted to with such force, and tonight, in this hotel, with this beautiful, beautiful man, it was not the champagne that reduced her inhibitions but the vibe of him, the presence that seeped into her pores, into her brain, and made her giddy with lust and with promise. It made twenty-four hours seem an impossible delay.

She had left for some privacy, to gather her thoughts, to convince herself she could hold out till tomorrow, but there was almost relief when she heard the door and his footsteps coming up behind her.

She felt the lips on the back of her neck and it felt like salvation, and she closed her eyes because all she wanted was to feel the tease of his mouth. He kissed her very slowly, and she felt the scratch of his unshaven jaw as lips slid across her flesh. She could stop him at any moment, his kiss so slow, so light, she could brush him off and turn around and pretend perhaps that it had never happened, except she gripped harder to the balcony wall and did not turn around, for she did not want it to end.

He kissed her harder, as if to warn her perhaps, as if to tell her she could end it here, but she wanted him more than she wanted a neat conclusion.

She wanted the hands that snaked around and slid to her stomach, she wanted the bruise she was sure he was leaving because he kissed low on her neck, so deep she felt like crying, felt like turning her head right round to suck on his mouth, but still she stood there. She wanted, how she wanted, the slight pressure on his fingers, the push back into him that gave her a daring feel of what was waiting, his solid length pressing into her bottom.

'We could take dessert upstairs,' Zander said, for he wanted her in his room. He wanted every morsel now that went into her mouth, every sip, to come only from him, everything to be untainted by his brother.

'I shouldn't.' Still she could not face him, still she dared not open her eyes, because if she did, she must make decisions, and she struggled so hard to remember. 'I'm working.'

'Not now,' Zander said. 'You just clocked off.'

'Your brother—'

'Forget about him,' Zander said, for he must be dismissed from this moment. Zander must not for a second reveal the bitterness that was there or she would run.

'I don't want to regret this in the morning.' It was a plea almost, because around him she could not think.

'Why would you regret something so nice?'

'Because…' she attempted, except his fingers were at the back of her bra and nimbly, easily, through her dress he unhooked her, and she was dressed except she felt naked, exposed. Shamelessly it exhilarated her. What did this man do? He turned her round and he gave her his mouth. He wrapped her in the heat of his arms and cooled her with his tongue. He kissed her, but Charlotte could never, she realised, recall it afterwards as just a kiss, for it stroked and it soothed and it beat in her mouth and dragged at her skin and it was faint-making and delicious and did things to her body that no mere kiss ever could. Even wearing her high heels he was the taller, and their bodies meshed. He pulled her right in, he leant on the balcony so his body was a curve for hers to melt into—and readily she did.

He gave all to that kiss and Zander had kissed many,

many women. Had kissed through his youth to assure a bed that night, had kissed just to get dinner when his stomach had been hollow with hunger, had kissed just to survive, but never, not once, had a kiss tasted so good.

Her lipstick was gone, her inhibitions fading, her breasts pressed against him, he caressed her. His mouth adored her in a way that made her feel both reckless and safe.

He took her away with his kiss and then he brought her back with its absence. He handed her her bag, which told her he had come out to fetch her; he draped her in her wrap and covered the swell of nipples beneath her dress, looked into her blue eyes and told her, looked right into them and told her, 'You'll never regret this.'

And he lied.

CHAPTER FIVE

WHY she trusted him she did not know.

Why she so willingly let him lead her to his room was not something she could readily explain.

In the bathroom of his luxury suite, she attempted to scold herself—to tell herself she knew nothing about this man, that he was a client of her boss, that she had known him for just a couple of days.

Not a single lecture worked.

He was the brother of Nico, whom she trusted, but it came down to something rather more basic than that, for there was no man on earth who made her feel the way Zander had in the time they had spent together.

She had not laughed so freely in years, had not talked so readily to another soul—and as for his kiss…

As she rinsed her mouth and looked up into her glittering eyes in the mirror, lifted the hair and saw the bruise he had left, she was also deeply honest with herself—in their few hours of contact he had offered escape. Tonight she was the dress and the shoes and the woman who looked back in the mirror, a woman who *could* handle things, she told herself as she removed her unhooked bra through the arms of her dress.

It was not love she sought as she walked from the bathroom to the lounge of his suite, it was escape and Zander offered it in spades.

Dessert had been delivered as loosely promised.

Shot glasses filled with mousses and brûlées, tiny pastries and potent custards, and not for a second was she tempted, at least not by the table, for she walked to him and was pulled down to his lap, to a kiss that did not need now to be tamed.

It was not the real Charlotte that kissed him back, it was the Charlotte she wanted to be, perhaps the Charlotte he thought he had met on the beach, a woman who could handle such things, could take the roaming of his hands on her body, could give her all and remember not to love him tomorrow.

For Zander, unusually, there was much at stake.

Wrongly, he assumed she had been his brother's lover and it was imperative he win before they met.

How delicious the moan in her throat as she sat on his knee and kissed him.

Did he do this? he wanted to ask as he tore down her dress to the breasts he had undressed and suckled at her nipples.

Or this? he begged in his head and stood with her in his lap and pushed her to the bed with his mouth.

Or this? As he slid down her panties.

There was a rough edge to his kisses, an urgency to him that hadn't been there before, an anger almost, and she pulled back on the bed, confused at the change in him.

'Zander?'

And he looked up to blue eye that held his, and saw her eyes were darker when troubled. He wanted them pale, wanted her soothed, wanted their night, not the conquest.

Wanted her.

'I've been thinking of you for so long,' he offered by way of explanation for his urgency. 'For weeks. Forgive me if I got carried away.' And he watched as she blinked, still wary. 'When we spoke, when you were in London and I was in Australia, when you were in bed…' And she blinked again, for she had thought of him too. Unable to picture him then, still her mind had wandered, so much so that she could now understand his haste. 'We'll take things slowly.' He smiled his lethal smile, except this time he meant it—thought not of his brother or hate, only of her. 'We'll go back to the beginning. How did you lie?'

She did not understand his question.

'How did you lie in your bed when you spoke with me?' And she could not help but smile at the memory of a dream that had come true, and could now forgive his roughness.

'On my side.'

'Show me.' He rose from the bed and she watched the suited man slowly undress as she rolled to her side and pulled up the covers around her shoulders.

'You?' Charlotte asked, as he climbed back into bed.

'On my back,' Zander said, and something deep in her stomach tightened. 'So tell me.'

'What?'

'How is the weather?'

And she lay on her side and closed her eyes and imagined the rain on her window and the grey of her life and his voice in her ear, only this time it was better, for it was cool but not cold in Xanos, and this time he was beside her.

'What did you do today?' This time, as she spoke of her day, she didn't have to pretend, didn't have to make anything up, for it was all real.

'I went walking in the hills.'

'Alone?' Zander asked.

'No, not alone.'

'And did you enjoy it?' This time, when she retold her day, there was his hand on her waist, this time and for evermore she would lie in her bed in her room and remember the feel of him, gentler hands now exploring her body, the nuzzle of his mouth on her arms along her shoulders, a tender exploration of her breast. 'Did you enjoy being with him in the hills?'

'Very much.'

'What did the two of you do?'

'We just kissed,' Charlotte said, as he rolled her onto her back.

'Just?' Zander asked, his mouth moving down to her stomach.

'Better than just.'

'Better than this?' he asked, and his head moved lower.

Though determined as his quest was to rise above Nico, as he tasted her with his mouth, he forgot to hate. Charlotte lay there, eyes open to the ceiling, to what should feel strange and wrong and unfamiliar, except as his tongue explored and his lips teased, he knew what she wanted as only a lover could; he knew more than her as he pushed down hips that were resisting and demanded she come to his mouth. He kissed her till she bore no more reluctance, till she gave to his mouth a part of her that had once been subdued.

And then, when her body was quiet, he rose over her and kissed her again, kissed her slowly till she was waking, till she was again alive with greedy want, could attune to different sensations. She wanted to feel him, to hold him, to sheath him, for his fingers were now within her and she wanted the rest.

Her fingers were all thumbs at the feel of him, the hard strength that would soon be within her, but his fingers were far more skilled than hers.

He felt the restraint of the latex, felt her clumsy roll down and wanted, for the first time, to tell her not to bother, wanted to really feel the intimate skin that wet his fingers now. Wanted more for himself than was usual as for Zander touching was merely a means to an end, the part where he said and did the right things, worked a while for a brief reward. Yet here and now this did not feel like work.

He forgot to hate for the first time, for it had no place in this room.

He forgot he was here to prove something, to claim something, as his body pressed towards her. He forgot too that he was performing, because that was all sex ever was, and he meant what he said as his fingers moved from inside her, as his erection moved to that place. What he said he would not recall, what she heard was in Greek and not fully understood, but it was an intimate declaration that did not require translation.

It was the words of a man moving deep into a woman he wanted.

She thought he would glide into her, so wet and ready was she, but Zander in full arousal did not make for soft landings, he slammed into soft tissue and stretched her completely. It was more compulsive than tender, a basic rhythm that was exquisite, and he took her breath away and did not let her catch it. When she wanted more, there was more; when she thought there could not be more, she was again proven wrong. He was in her body, in her head and in her heart as he gave everything and simultaneously demanded everything from her. She had never known hands roam so hungrily, or a tongue and a breath in her ear, or the sheen of his back beneath her fingers. There were too many sensations for Charlotte to focus on, so she did not try, just moved with him and beyond herself, moved to a place that was waiting for them.

He moaned and it made her feel dizzy; he moved faster and she did too, and there was a hush then, a moment of stillness, no work needed now, just a wait for arrival, and it was now that he glided, and flew her away. She felt every beat and responded with her own; she heard every breath and tasted his moan, and as their bodies quieted she went back in her head, closed her eyes and attempted to reel in her heart.

It was too soon to love him.

They did not sleep for ages; they tried not to sleep. Zander could see the red numbers on the clock that ticked beside them, their hours left too few, not that she knew it. And here in his bed, with a woman beside him, for once he did not want to roll over, did not want to escape to sleep, or order from the bar, or envision tomorrow. For the first time he was comfortable in a place.

'What is it like?' She lay there and tried to fathom it, to comprehend how it must have been for him, and though she had said not to discuss things, it was way too late for that now. 'What is it like knowing that you have a twin and never having seen him?'

'I have seen him,' Zander said, for he was not sure if it was a memory or if it was the one photo he had found, but he had seen his brother, they had once been together. 'When we were babies…' He did not want to talk about it, did not need to explain it. He turned to his side and closed his eyes, but she turned too, her hand loose on his waist, her breath on his back. He held his breath for if he did not he would speak, would ask her to leave, for suddenly she felt too close.

'I mean…' Still she would not leave it, did not heed the silent warning to halt. 'What was it like, growing up without him? What has it been like, knowing you have an identical twin?'

And maybe there was weakness, for already it was tomorrow, already the day was here. Maybe it was sex that made him soften, or maybe it was her voice that sounded more tender than probing, or her hand that still stayed on his waist, because he did not tell her to be silent, did not respond in the way that he usually would have; instead, he lay in the silence as she patiently awaited his response and he thought about it.

He actually thought about it and how best to describe it.

'You look in the mirror each morning?' He was grateful that she did not answer with the obvious 'Yes', that she let him be for another moment with his thoughts. 'Imagine looking and there is no reflection, knowing there is a you that you cannot see.'

And he could explain it no better, and he did not try to.

There was no point anyway.

Tomorrow, when she knew him, she might not want him in her life.

CHAPTER SIX

WAKING up in a strange bed, a strange country, should have had Charlotte in a complete panic, but she did not feel as if it was a stranger who lay beside her.

She watched him sleep and admired his beauty, her body lazy but still in arousal from the feel of his solid weight beside her through the night. Now, with the sun slowly waking Xanos, she got to watch him in colour. His skin, pale in the predawn light, glowed a smooth olive in the sun, and she gazed at the full, sensuous mouth that had explored her so intimately, had to resist moving over to kiss those lips; instead, she lay on her side and admired, saw the shadows to his stomach lift and reveal an ebony snake of hair. How she wanted to move that sheet, to see all of him.

He must have felt her eyes on him because he woke to find her watching, woke to the day he had long been awaiting, but he did not want to get out of bed. He looked at Charlotte and he wanted to stay, he wanted to pull her towards him, to bury his head in her hair, to make love in the morning, except that would be too cruel, even by his standards, for he knew what was about to come.

He did not move so she did, slid over the bed and kissed him because she still trusted in last night, in all they had found. Even as his mouth resisted, she did not question why. Still she kissed him. And he let her. She kissed him and he found himself kissing her back till there was a reluctant return, a recall to last night, to remember the intimacy they had shared that had gone way beyond sex, and Zander recoiled from her as he remembered just how close he had come to confiding in her. He did what he always did in the morning—instead of lingering, he climbed out of bed.

'I have to get ready.'

She heard and felt his dismissal, despite his appropriate words, for the clock was already nearing seven.

'So do I.' She pulled on her dress, readied herself for the shameful lift ride in last night's clothes. She could face it if he said farewell with a smile or a kiss that told her there was still tonight.

Neither was forthcoming.

'Good luck for today.'

'I never rely on luck' came his curt response.

'When I see you, when I speak with Nico—'

'We never met,' Zander said, and Charlotte nodded, for it did make things easier with her boss.

He was nervous about meeting Nico, about seeing his twin after all these years, Charlotte told herself as she headed to her room, and she was nervous too as she dressed in a smart navy suit and because of the bruise wore her hair down. Then she headed to the meeting rooms she had booked. She did a slight double-take when Nico walked in, a crisper, more clean-cut version of the man she had been in bed with last night, and, yes, she felt guilt, not for the act but towards her boss.

'I'm sorry to hear about your father,' she offered. 'How is he?'

'Extremely unwell,' Nico responded. 'After this meeting, I must go directly to the hospital—I trust that has been arranged?'

'Of course,' Charlotte said. 'I've cancelled the rest of your week. Do you need me to clear things further?'

'Not at this stage.' There was a pause, a long one, and she knew she must fill it, must do the right thing by Nico, for after all he was her boss. Unable to look him in the face properly, she wished this morning was over, that the surprise was revealed and that Nico knew, and then she could see where that left her and Zander. 'Nico…' God, how much to tell him? 'About this meeting. I know how important getting this land is to you. The thing is—'

'In the scheme of things it is not that important,' Nico interrupted. 'I have not come away from my dying father about a piece of land. There's something I need to tell you.' Nico, as always, was direct. 'I was going to explain things to you, except my father got ill. Still, I should have warned you, for had you bumped into him you would have got a shock…' She froze as Nico spoke on. 'This meeting today could get very personal. I just want to prepare you. You see, when I found out I had been adopted, I also found out that I had a twin. Zander. The businessman you have been dealing with is actually Alexandros Kargas…'

Her face flew to Nico's, her mind torn in two as if it were paper as she tried not to reveal that she knew already, tried to fathom how Nico did.

'When did you find out?'

'Just recently. I had no idea that the landowner was him, of course, but now that I do, it makes sense.' Nico was grim. 'I think he is hoping to shock me.'

'To surprise you?' Charlotte forced a smile, but it died when Nico shook his head.

'Yes, though I don't think he's planning a pleasant one. Fortunately I am one step ahead of him. There is a lot of history, Charlotte, none of it relevant to you. Suffice it to say the difficulties in reaching him these past weeks, well, it has nothing to do with a piece of land—he has been baiting me.'

'Baiting you?'

But, of course, Nico did not have to explain things to her. 'I just want you to be prepared that there may be a confrontation this morning, that there will be raised voices. On no account are you to come in or panic and call for assistance. I am expecting trouble and I am prepared for it.' He headed into the meeting room and she was left with racing thoughts. Taking a seat at the desk outside, she placed her head in her hands, tried to work out from the last couple of days if what Nico was saying was true. She went over and over the conversations between Zander and her and wondered if he had been quizzing her, but all she had witnessed had been kindness. Surely Nico had got things wrong?

Paulo too?

They were wrong, she was sure of it. And when Zander walked towards the meeting room, Charlotte turned worried eyes to him, for had she not been in bed with him last night, had she not been held by him, had she not witnessed his tenderness first hand? But, then, every presumption Nico had uttered rang true, for the only word that could describe Zander's appearance this morning was savage. Charlotte saw him in a suit for the first time, exquisitely tailored in the darkest of greys. He might have been dressed for a funeral, his tie a slate grey and that jet hair slicked back; he still had not shaved and somehow it spelt insolence. Her eyes begged for reassurance when they met his, and she willed from him a brief smile, a wink, some private reference to last night, to the knowledge that it would all be okay, but instead her eyes met those of a stranger.

'Is he in?'

It was all he asked, all he wanted from her, and when she nodded he swept past her desk, gave one sharp knock on the door, and did not wait for Nico to respond. He opened the door and walked straight in, and all Charlotte glimpsed before the door closed was Nico standing straight to meet his twin for the first time.

Thank God Nico had warned her as to how she should react, for though there were no really raised voices, there was a brutality to the words that were muffled by the walls. Then there was a scrape of furniture that, had she not been told to ignore it, would have had Charlotte ringing her boss to ensure that all was okay.

And she waited for it to be so.

She waited for it to be the surprise reunion Zander had assured that it would be, except it appeared the meeting was to go down as Nico had feared.

The door opened. Zander went to march out and then harsh words were hurled from Nico, and there were no walls or door now to muffle his anger, no barrier to deflect the strength behind his words.

'I will not leave Xanos.' She had never heard her boss so angry. 'I will stay here as long as I choose. There is still much to find out.'

'I've told you all you need to know.' She saw Zander turn, his back so taut she saw the stretch of the fabric that struggled to contain muscles that had rippled beneath her fingers last night. She wanted to stop him, wanted to rush over, but she knew it was not her place, knew even then that she had been deceived, especially as Zander spoke on. 'There will never be a relationship. I do not have a brother, or a mother. You left me with him and now you return—'

'As if I had a choice!' Nico's shout matched Zander's but his hate did not, for Zander was so full of loathing Charlotte could almost taste it.

'You lived your rich, pampered life away from Xanos. Now you return like some grandiose prodigal son… But you are not wanted,' Zander said. 'You do not belong here. I will build that nightclub, so enjoy the noise of machinery, for it will be nothing compared to the music that will pound in your home night after night…'

'For what purpose?' Nico demanded.

'Misery.' Zander's answer was simple. 'Touch my things, encroach on my life and I will make it my business to ensure the rest of yours is miserable.'

But Nico still had questions.

'What do you know—' so badly he need closure '—about our mother? Do you know if she lives?'

'She is dead to me,' Zander said. 'She was dead to me the day she chose you. Go find her if you must, show her the son she saved.'

'She did not save me,' Nico shouted at his brother. 'She sold me!'

'No!' Zander's roar was absolute, for only Zander had lived his life, only Zander knew the hell of being the one left behind—and he'd have rather have been sold to the devil than be left a single day with that man who bore the title of father. 'She saved you—so bask in it, *brother.*' He sneered the word. 'But get the hell away from Xanos, and keep the hell away from me.'

She sat, more at stake than her boss must ever realise, and as Zander swept out she had to resist leaping to her feet. She wanted to demand what had gone wrong with his plans, why Nico was so furious, or was it Zander?

For Zander it should now be over. He had said all he had come to say, yet it did not sate his anger. Still there was a burn in his guts, a need for more. Adrenaline still flooded his muscles, had his heart pounding in his throat with such force he wanted to rip off his tie and tear at his shirt. He was furious that his twin had known, that Nico had stood and faced him as he'd walked in rather than recoil in shock. Insulted by Nico's outstretched hand, Zander had declined it; instead, he had told him exactly his feelings—that there would be no contact, that forgiveness would never be on the table. That his mother had chosen the golden one, had given Nico the chance of a privileged life and left Zander to survive for himself.

And he had.

Oh, he had.

He did not need anyone.

He had made it alone and would go on doing so.

Would destroy Nico if he tried to get close.

And, now that was over, all he wanted was to get out.

Away from the man who looked like him, away from the reflection that was now in his mirror.

Away from the son that his mother had chosen.

And then, as he strode out, when he would have preferred to hit, or to run, he saw her sitting there, saw the confusion in her eyes and the tremble to the mouth that last night had been his. And he did not want her for Nico, he wanted her for himself.

'Get your things.' He snapped his fingers to tell her his haste. He wanted her away, he wanted her upstairs, he wanted her on his bed, and he would forget what he had just seen, forget the brother that never would be, he would lose himself in her. But she just sat there.

'Get your things!' Zander said. 'You come with me.'

He did not understand her hesitation. He was offering her his world, offering more of what they had had last night. 'You work for me now,' he clarified, except Nico was walking out of his office and still Charlotte sat there.

'Charlotte has nothing to do with this,' Nico said.

'Except that she comes now with me,' Zander retorted, without looking at the man he loathed. 'Come now.' He gave her one more chance when he gave others none but, pale, she still sat there, her eyes moving from his to Nico and then back to him.

'I work for Nico.' Her voice was as pale as her face.

'My staff are loyal to me,' came his brother's voice, and Zander could not believe that she would choose him after the night they had shared. His mind was so black with loathing, so angry having lived a life of betrayal, that there was no chance of straight thinking.

'Really?' Zander shot back. 'Well, that's not how it seemed when her legs were wrapped around me last night.' It all came out in one caustic response. Zander watched her quail as the words spewed out, but really the words were not aimed at provoking her and he looked at Nico to relish his response. He wanted his brother to thump him; he wanted a fist because it was pain he could see, a bruise he could feel, hurt that could be measured. He wanted to fight but his brother just stood there, and, worse, Charlotte apologised for the one good thing on Xanos that had ever taken place.

'I'm sorry, Nico…' She could not have felt more betrayed, more humiliated, more ashamed—could so clearly see now how she had been used. She could not stand to look at Zander, so she looked at her boss instead. He was the man she should have been loyal to, the man who paid her wages. 'I'm so sorry, Nico.'

'No problem.' Nico was tough, and could be just as cutting as his brother, though the barb in his response, she knew, was not aimed at her. 'We're all allowed a mistake—yours just happened to be my brother.'

CHAPTER SEVEN

She lay curled up and wounded on the bed, too morti-fied to go out, dreading Nico's wrath, but far more than that she was beyond hurt by what Zander had done.

The contempt, the disregard, how he had used her.

A knock at the door a short while later did not see Charlotte moving. She did not care who it might be: Nico to fire her or Zander, for what?

An apology wasn't going to fix this.

Instead, when the knock came again, she closed her eyes at the sound of a woman's voice.

'Charlotte, it's me—Constantine.'

She could not be rude to Nico's wife. She had met her a few times and Constantine had always been nice. Beyond ashamed, Charlotte opened the door, and burst into tears when the other woman wrapped her arms around her.

'Nico told me what happened.'

'I'm so sorry,' Charlotte wept. 'I'm so ashamed…'

'For what?'

'For what I did.' Everything that had been so beau-tiful had been turned around and it all seemed sullied and sordid now. 'I thought…I never thought he hated Nico. It was not about being disloyal.'

'Charlotte.' Constantine was kind. 'What happened between you and Zander is not Nico's business, or mine.'

'It has become that though,' Charlotte wept. 'I really thought…' But she could not divulge her dreams because they seemed so pathetic now, that with one look, with one kiss, he had whisked her away, had let her glimpse a world she did not know and now wished she never had.

'Is Nico going to fire me?'

'He wants to speak with you, he wants to know what was said, what Zander revealed. I doubt he could fire you for sleeping with someone.' Constantine gave a wry smile. 'My husband is many things, but he is never a hypocrite. He is cross,' she admitted, 'furious, but I think that is more aimed at his brother. As I pointed out to him when he told me what had happened, we were together the night we met—it was, in fact, my wedding night and Nico was not the groom…' Charlotte blinked at the admission from Nico's wife. 'I know how devastating they can be, how irresistible Nico was to me. I am not here to judge you, I just want to know you are okay.'

'I will be,' Charlotte said, for she was certainly not okay now. She tried to scan her future for a time when this would not hurt so much, but Zander had changed it for ever. 'If I had thought, for even a second, that he was not looking forward to meeting Nico… Why would he hate him? It's not as if Nico was raised by his parents. Nico was the one that was sold...'

'Roula, their mother, she was not stable...' Constantine paused. Charlotte could see the other woman was uncomfortable discussing this, for though Charlotte had been privy to certain information, emotion had always been left out, only names and facts had been given by Nico. 'Or that is what we have been told. She left the father and worked the streets... The Eliadeses desperately wanted a baby...' Constantine screwed her eyes closed, and it was clear that she hated discussing this. 'Alexandros, I mean Zander, was raised by his father. It would seem...' Charlotte closed *her* eyes as Constantine spoke on and she recalled Zander telling her that his time in Xanos had not all been happy. 'He was not a good man, he was a cruel man, in fact.'

'If that was the case, why would she leave Zander with him?'

'That is what we are trying to find out. There are so many questions, which is why we are searching for her. But Zander has run true to form, it would seem—like father, like son.'

Charlotte's eyes opened at the rare bitterness in Constantine's voice and though she was hurting, bleeding inside, even though she had nothing to base it on, something within her rose to defend him. 'You can't say that.'

'Oh, but I can,' Constantine flared. 'He has done nothing to prove otherwise. Cruel seems a very good word to describe him to me. He has bought up the homes on the island for a pittance and now, till he is ready to bulldoze them, he rents them out for a small fortune, at least it is a fortune to the locals. He's building a nightclub and there is talk of a casino, yet he does not give the locals the work. He wants my husband and son to leave Xanos, and will do anything to engineer it, even ruin the rest of the island just to get his way.'

'It's business,' Charlotte attempted. 'Maybe when he has calmed down… It must have been unnerving to finally meet his twin.'

'He has no nerves to unnerve' was Constantine's swift response. Was that pity in her eyes as she looked at Charlotte? 'How can you defend him after what he just did to you? If it is only in business that he is cruel, what does that make you?'

Her words were like a slap and Charlotte retracted as if hit.

'I don't want him to hurt you further, Charlotte, but he will if you let him.'

'I won't give him the opportunity.' Of that she was sure, but still she knew her own mind, would not be silenced because it suited Constantine. 'But you're wrong, Constantine. If it comes down to like father like son, what does that make Nico?'

'He was not raised by him.'

'No, he was raised by a man who bought him, who lied even when confronted with the truth.' This much at least Charlotte knew and she watched Constantine's flushed, angry cheeks pale a little. 'Zander is not all bad,' Charlotte said. He couldn't be. He simply could not be, for she remembered them walking on the beach. He was the only man to touch her soul. She remembered their day and she remembered his smile and the rare sound of his laughter. In a second, as she sat on the bed wounded with hurt, her heart forced recall, told her that despite evidence to the contrary, their time together, their day, their night had surely not all been contrived, had not all been a lie. Her heart told her so.

'You need to be careful when dealing with him,' Constantine warned.

'I'm having no dealings with him,' Charlotte replied, and then realised what Constantine was saying. 'I still have a job?' She thought of her mother, of all the balls she was juggling back home, and when Constantine hesitated, the surge of hope faded, but Constantine took her hands.

'You have to do it, though. Nico needs you to stay here for a few days to go through his itinerary. He is heading back to the hospital soon to spend some time with his father, but though Zander has made things difficult, some things just can't be put on hold. He wants to see you downstairs in the restaurant for a meeting. He wants to up the search for his mother and, no matter what, he wants that land.'

'I can't face Zander.' Charlotte could not go out there—she simply could not go out there.

'But face him you must.' Constantine was resolute. It was her little family under attack from Zander after all and, as kind as she had been to Charlotte, on this there was no compromise. 'You work for Nico—don't forget that again.'

CHAPTER EIGHT

'CHARLOTTE, please...'

Just when her heart could surely not be more torn, she answered the phone to the sobs of her mother. 'When are you coming to get me?'

Charlotte closed her eyes. 'I'm at work, Mum.'

'You said you'd never leave me.'

'I'm sorry about this.' A nurse came on the line. 'We have a residents' phone...'

'Mum's got my number in her diary.' Charlotte closed her eyes. 'Is she okay?'

'She's taking a little while to orientate, but most of the time she's fine. It's just every now and then she gets into a panic. It often happens with temporary residents. She'll settle in in a couple of days.'

And then it would be time to take her home. Charlotte thought of the battle that lay ahead, of the increased confusion that awaited, of the impossibility of it all, but she could not think of that now. Getting through the morning was proving a difficult enough task, let alone looking to the future.

'Can you put her back on to speak with me, please?'

Charlotte spoke with her mother for a few moments, reassuring Amanda that she was at work and that her stay at the home was only temporary, but the call depleted her already shot nerves.

Shaky hands applied lip gloss and she put drops in her swollen eyes. Charlotte was nervous and embarrassed to be facing Nico, but more than that dreaded that she might see Zander, and wondered how on earth she should react to him if she did. But surely he had checked out, Charlotte consoled herself. After all, he had said his piece to his brother, had made it clear that he would not be selling the land and wanted nothing to do with him whatsoever. What reason could he have to be here? She attempted to reassure herself, trying to ignore the fact that he practically owned the south of Xanos and had *every* reason to stay for a few days at the very least.

Somehow she had to tell Nico that she was not able to stay any longer on Xanos, that she had to get home. But how could she possibly assert herself after what had just taken place? Of all the stupid things to do with Zander, of all the blind, stupid things. Nico was hardly going to accept demands from her now when by her own actions she had suddenly become extremely dispensable.

Damn you, Zander!

It was a relief to be angry.

A welcome change from guilt and remorse and shame. In fact, so angry was Charlotte that as she stepped out of the lift and headed across the foyer to the restaurant, to the table where Nico waited, instead of burning in a blush when she saw Zander sitting on the other side of the restaurant, looking up from the paper he was reading and sipping on coffee as if he did not have a care, instead of looking hurriedly away, she positively glowered at him. Her anger forced her to hold her head high as she crossed the room and joined her boss.

Nico had ordered two coffees—a milky one for Charlotte and a short black for himself. He gave a very tight smile as she approached. 'Well,' Nico said as she took a seat at the table. 'This is awkward.' He was as direct as ever and so honest with the circumstances that it made her smile, even made her laugh just a little as Nico rolled his eyes, but her smile soon faded. 'You should have told me you had spoken with Zander—you should have informed me that you had met him.'

'I know,' Charlotte said. 'I tried.'

'I know that you tried to call, and that you found out my father was ill.' Nico stirred sugar into his coffee, but even as she entered into the most difficult of conversations, her shoulder was burning, for she could feel Zander watching them. 'But, still, you should have said when you spoke with Constantine.' She was shamed by the pity in Nico's eyes now when he looked at her. 'I could have warned you what he is like.'

'You knew?' She was determined not to cry, not in front of Nico and certainly not with Zander close by, but, damn it, it was hard to sit there and have it confirmed just how easily she had been used. 'You knew that his intentions were not good?'

'When you rang and said that the owner was coming, that Zander…' Nico grimaced for it had been a painful realisation for him too. 'I went and got the house deeds, saw his signature and, call it twin intuition, I knew there was trouble brewing. I knew that Zander knew who I was, that he was coming to confront me.'

'I believed him when he said it would be a surprise.'

'You listen only to me now,' Nico warned. 'Your loyalty is only to me.'

And she nodded, because it had to be now, because Zander had let her down so badly. All their time together had been a sham of his making.

'What did he tell you?' Nico asked. 'Did he speak about our parents?'

'No.' She raked her mind back over their conversations, realised just how much he had avoided talking about himself. 'He gave nothing away.'

'He must have revealed something?' Nico urged. 'You met him on Saturday. Surely you spoke, not just…' He held his tongue and she was grateful, for they had not just tumbled into bed.

'We spoke a lot.'

'Did he say anything about our mother?'

'Nothing, just that he had never met her.'

'Charlotte?'

'That was it. He said that his time here on Xanos was not all happy.' And even if Zander had betrayed her in the vilest of ways, still she could not do the same to him, could not tell Nico about the markets and the thieving, about the taverna and the memories he had shared. She was sure, quite sure, Nico didn't need to know that. Already Constantine had said they knew the father was a brute. 'Nico, he told me nothing. He was using me to get information, not the other way around, and I told him nothing. Despite the mistakes I have made over the weekend, I was not indiscreet about you.'

He accepted that, and for that she was grateful. 'I need you to stay on in Xanos—perhaps into next week. I want you to look into the licensing for the club he is talking about building, just get some research together, and I have a lead on my mother. I need you to ring around, perhaps fly out to the mainland and visit a few homes.' He looked up. 'I trust that is not a problem.'

So badly she wanted to say that it was the most terrible problem, that she needed to get back to her mother, that travel was impossible, but the reality was that right now she needed a job, needed to pay for the bill that would come in for the nursing home, needed the wages that Nico paid. Cold reality beckoned in a way that it never had before. She needed this job, needed to work even if that might mean her mother had to live permanently in the home. It would be far easier to sit and weep now, but instead she forced her voice to be casual, even managed to look Nico in the eye as she spoke. 'Of course it's not.'

'And I want that land,' Nico said. 'I am not moving my wife and child from Xanos at his bidding. If he accepts my offer, you are to get it immediately in writing.'

'I am to deal with him?' That she could not handle.

'Of course.' Nico frowned. 'Though you will deal

with him rather more professionally this time, I hope.'
And he asked her again. 'Is that a problem?'

She knew what Nico was doing, knew that even if
he was giving her a chance to redeem herself, he also
saw her as a link to his brother. If she had had any en-
ergy left, she would have argued her case, but instead
Charlotte sat there, knew when she was beaten.

'No, it won't be a problem.'

Nico stood. 'Charlotte, I'm trusting you to do the
right thing.' She nodded, and closed her eyes. In a rare
move, Nico put a hand on her shoulder and gave it a
small squeeze, for he was more disappointed than angry.
Perhaps even a little guilty, for his private life had now
impacted badly on her and, yes, he did want her to find
out some more. 'All will be fine.'

Zander sat, watching his brother's hand on her shoulder, watching her back to him, watching the man he
hated most give Charlotte comfort. He knew she needed
comfort because of him, and it caused something to stir
inside as he recalled his words, recalled the gasp that
had come from her lips and the shock on her face.

His richly blended coffee tasted like acid as it slid
down his throat. There was a burn in his stomach and
a clench in his scalp as his brother walked past, as Nico
had the gall to give him a brief nod.

He did not want a polite greeting, did not want to
foster anything with him. Yet the eyes that had looked
in his direction felt like his own, the face, the walk—it
was like looking in the mirror, except different. Looking
at a reflection that was a better version of himself.

He looked over to where Charlotte remained and usually Zander did not entertain guilt, considered it a wasted emotion, an expensive emotion—but he could see her rigid posture. She turned her head and smiled as Nico said goodbye to her, and then he watched her shoulders drop, just a fraction, but he could see the internal collapse, see her hand tremble as she picked up her coffee, see her try to right herself, to sit up straight again, and then, when it didn't work, he watched as she stood to leave. He could see her eyes avoiding him as she walked across the restaurant. 'Charlotte.' He called her name, and of course she ignored him. He caught her wrist as she brushed past. 'Join me.'

'Join you!' She could not believe his audacity. It was way too soon to attempt professional. Surely she would be given a day's grace at the very least before she had to deal with him. 'Nico is still here. If you have business to discuss I can arrange—'

'I do not want to speak with him.'

'Then I can get Paulo…' She was having great trouble talking, could feel his fingers scalding her wrist. She wanted to slap him, to pick up his coffee and toss it in his lap, to hand back even an ounce of the hurt that he had landed her with, but Nico had spelt out the rules. Nico, she realised in that hopeless moment as she stood there, was using her too for she was, for now, the link to Zander, the pawn, the plaything that might make him linger, the trinket Zander wanted, perhaps for a while. She stood and remembered, remembered his cruel words, how he had sneered that her legs had been wrapped around him. And she didn't just hear his words, she saw the vision too, was back there in the passionate moments, remembering how deeply he had kissed her, how much he had ravished her, how pliant her body had been in arms, how good the bastard was, and it took everything she possessed just to stand there as his words were delivered.

'I don't want to speak with Paulo. I discuss business with you.'

'But you don't want to discuss business.'

'Of course I do. There are some questions I have about his future use of the land—and about the maintenance of the jetty.' He smiled and it lacerated. He lied and it killed her that he did.

'I'm a PA,' Charlotte said. 'It's not my job—'

'I choose who I liaise with. If you choose not to, then go and tell your boss that you refuse to speak with me.' He let go of her wrist then, for he knew she could not run. He snapped his fingers at a passing waiter and told him to organise a meeting room now, and it was said with such authority that the waiter immediately put down the plate he was carrying and Charlotte stood trembling, waiting as a room was hastily arranged. All she knew was that she did not want to be alone with him, did not trust him. Neither did she trust herself, for as they were led through the foyer her legs were like liquid.

They passed the bar where they had so recently sat together, where he had pressed his leg into her. How he must have inwardly been laughing. She glanced at the restaurant and the balcony beyond, where he had so skilfully seduced her. They turned to the function rooms, and into one of them. The slam of the door behind her told her why she was so very afraid, for she was back in his space, back alone with him, and for all he had done, still there was want.

Want as he turned to face her, want as he walked over to where she stood, her shoulders back against the door, want as she tried to be free of him, want for the man she had thought she had met.

'What I said about us to Nico—'

'Cannot be erased by an apology,' Charlotte cut in, for she must keep her head, must remember that it had all been a ruse, a lie, that she knew nothing about the man who stood before her now. 'You were right with what you said this morning—we never met. You're not the man I thought I knew, so let's just deal with the paperwork. I don't need to hear your feigned apology.'

'Why would I apologise?' She could not believe his audacity. 'I was offering you a job—a far better one than you have, working for him.'

'You really think that I'd ever work for you?' She could not, *could not*, believe what she was hearing. 'After what you did, you really think that I'd consider—?'

'I would pay you more than Nico does.'

'It's not about money.'

'What, then?' Zander asked. 'You prefer to be his mistress? To share him with his wife?'

She did slap him then, professional or not. A morning's worth of hurt leapt down her arm and was delivered by her palm and slammed into his cheek. He did not even flinch, he just stood there, then gave her a black smile as, stunned by her own actions, by the venom of her thoughts, she shrank against the door. *This* was what he had made her.

'I work for Nico,' she said through pale lips, 'because he is a wonderful boss. Because he has integrity, because I trust him, because he has never, and would never, expect what you clearly would from me. I could never work for you and I will never, ever sleep with you again.'

'You did not object last night.'

'Last night you seduced me.' She could see it so clearly now. 'Last night you set out to—'

'Ah, *po po po…*' He spoke in Greek, and she knew enough of the language to get his meaning, and it burned that he could tut, tut, tut away the night they had shared, could be so condescending about something that had been so wondrous. She felt as if she were back on the hillside with him, but with clarity now, could hear the birds calling, for war had already been declared, he just hadn't thought to tell her.

Charlotte had to bite on her lip for a moment to catch her voice, for she would speak her truth without breaking down and her voice rose as she forced herself to continue. 'Last night you let me think it was about me, that it was about us, when, in fact, you had another agenda entirely.' Her hand stung from the contact with him, her palm burnt red and she raked it through her hair to cool it, to wipe herself clean from him. He watched a moment as the blonde curtain lifted and he saw the bruise that his mouth had made, a visible reminder, proof of what had taken place; but the curtain fell and still the image remained, not of purple on pale flesh but the feel of her skin beneath his lips, how she had melted to him, how right they had been, how close he had come to sharing with another person, how she had been his. 'You really tell me you have not slept with Nico…'

'You have no right to ask me that!' And she hadn't, but her past was her own and certainly not for sharing with him. Still, she could not stay quiet, remembered now his push to the bed, and that it had not been just lust for her that had driven him. 'Did it turn you on, thinking that I had, Zander?' There was a warrior inside, a woman who rose, who would not let him destroy her, and she found her and moved from the door towards him, challenged him when it would have been so much easier to recoil. 'Did you like the idea, Zander, that you were better, that you made me come harder?' She taunted him as she reminded him because, damn, he deserved reminding about what he had done, what he had so readily destroyed. 'Well, you were wasting your time thinking about your brother—your mind should have been on me.'

'It was,' Zander said. 'I was not thinking of that.' The admission and the passion with which it was delivered surprised even him, because her words had taken him back there and, no, triumph over his brother had not been on his mind then; instead, it had all been her.

'It was *all* you were thinking of?' Charlotte sneered.

And he closed his eyes because, yes, at first it had been.

'Those little chats…' How it stung. How innocent she had been to lie in bed on a grey morning in London and listen to him, to recall how he had brightened her day, yet it had all been a game to him. How easily he had played her—how readily she had let him.

'I should have heeded the warnings.' She was furious not just at Zander but at herself, and then she threw back at him what Paulo had told her in Greek about his tawdry reputation, that he would sell his mother to the highest bidder, and she told him too how the islanders hated him.

'I am not here for a lecture from you.'

'Are you going to sign?' She just wanted out of there, she wanted away, she wanted done, or she would start crying.

'I have not decided.' He looked at her. 'Perhaps we go out on my yacht to discuss things, spend some time away…'

'Never,' Charlotte said.

'Never?' Zander checked.

'I hate you.'

'Tut tut.' Zander smiled. 'What would your boss say if he knew you were speaking to me like that? I thought Nico still wanted that land.'

'I'll resign before I have to spend a day with you.' She was trapped, completely trapped, and the slap she had delivered had not put out the fire inside, for it was flaring again, as it had done the whole wretched morning, building and building till it could not be contained. 'You have no idea what you've done to me. Because of you, I might have to put my mother in a home.' Which was perhaps a bit harsh, for it had been heading towards that for months now. It was hardly all his fault, but Zander had made it impossible to approach her boss at this moment, impossible to negotiate for a better arrangement, when she had let him down so badly, and the words tumbled out untamed.

'What are you talking about?' He sneered at the hysterical female who blamed a night of passion for every last ill, but something niggled inside Zander, something unfamiliar, for he had seen her so vibrant, so happy, and now she seemed to be choking with fury and fear almost. 'How can I be responsible for your mother's—?'

'Oh, what would you care about family?' Charlotte snapped, already regretting the words that had spilled out, wishing she could somehow sink to her knees and retrieve them, gather them up and put them in her bag and pretend they had never been said. But it was far too late for that now and the best she could do was look him briefly in the eye before walking out. She looked into black eyes that had once caressed her but were unrecognisable now. 'You're trying to destroy yours; I'm just trying to hold onto mine. What would you know about it?'

'The offer is there.' Zander would not enter a discussion on family, did not want to know of her ills. 'I will consider signing the papers *when* you decide to join me.'

CHAPTER NINE

SHE was his captor.

It felt absolutely like that.

The vast hotel felt like a goldfish bowl. Every time she turned, even if he wasn't there, she anticipated him.

The only relief was the occasional visit to nursing homes and hostels for the homeless on the mainland in the search for Roula Kargas. Nico's thorough search had already ruled out their mother being on Xanos or Lathira, but no matter how promising the lead, every time the result was same—the patient was too old, or the history wrong. Every time it was not their mother.

'Anything?' Nico asked when she rang early the next morning to report on her previous day, but they both knew it was bad news for had it been good she would immediately have told him. 'Nothing. Her name was right...' Charlotte gave a tense sigh. 'I thought I had found your mother, but she was from Rhodes, and the child she had given up was a girl. It was actually really sad.'

'I would have gone myself,' Nico explained. 'The trouble is, my father...' He did not need to explain further. Both knew there was little time left. The doctors were talking in hours now. 'I know that I am asking a lot from you, Charlotte, that this is not part of your more usual work, and it is much appreciated. You need to unwind. Ring the spa, it is world class. Have a massage…'

She might just do that. She could feel the knots in her neck, in her shoulders, in her jaw, even in her fingers that gripped the phone.

'Has Zander been in contact?'

'No.' She had told Nico about the offer to take her out on his boat and, though desperate for information, even Nico had agreed that would be too much to ask.

'If you do speak with him, though…' There was a rare pause from her boss, for their conversations were always brief. He always said what was needed and then hung up, except this was so personal and there was so much pain, it had shifted how things worked. 'I want to find my mother, Charlotte. Any clue, any information, no matter how small.'

'If he tells me anything, I shall pass it on.' She hung up the phone, cross with Nico, yet she could not blame him for his desperation to find out about his past.

She paced the room till she was sick of the walls and she stepped out to the balcony to breathe, to drag in some air, except there Zander was on his balcony, reading the newspaper, coffee in hand, and she raced back inside, only to hear a knock on the door. It couldn't be him, of course, given he was on his balcony, but her heart was thumping as she opened the door. The bellboy was hidden by a huge bunch of orchids and, on reading the attached card, an *apology* from Zander for any *indiscretions* and a summons, rather than an invitation, to join him for morning tea so that he could apologise in person. To add insult to injury, the florist had signed his name incorrectly.

Both card and flowers went in the bin.

Unless he contacted her about work, she would have nothing to do with him, Charlotte decided.

Indiscretions indeed! He was a brave man to request her presence.

The smell of orchids filled the room, but she refused to open the sliding doors, deciding instead that she *would* have the massage that Nico had suggested.

It was but a brief escape, although a pleasant one. Her body was smoothed and pummelled, oiled fingers massaged her scalp and she could almost feel the tension seeping out of her body and through her fingertips. As she was left alone for the lotions to work, as she lay in the warm, darkened room, her mind did not automatically drift to Zander, as it did all too often these days, for he was not the only problem she had. Neither did her thoughts drift to the constant worry about her mother. No, given this pause, for the first time in a long time there was a moment to focus on self, and the voice she had been silencing for a while now started to make itself known. It was a voice that was familiar from her childhood. It blamed others for her problems, heaped on the guilt—the voice of her mother was becoming her own and Charlotte did not like the sound of it a bit. Yes,

Zander had hurt her. Yes, his behaviour had been beyond appalling, but her problems were her own and she knew they needed to be sorted out rather than shelved, knew that so much had to change.

The massage both regenerated and soothed her, but it was a fix that Charlotte knew was only temporary for all too soon she was back in the lift, heading to her room. She swiped the card in her door, relieved to be inside, but her relief was short-lived for there he was, sitting on the chair. She didn't jump, for she put nothing past him.

'I'll complain.'

'To whom?' Zander said. 'I own the hotel.' He glanced over to the bin. 'I see that you don't like orchids.'

'I love orchids,' Charlotte said, 'or rather I used to.' She gave him a very tight smile. 'Though the scent of them will now forever make my stomach curl.'

'I asked you to join me in the restaurant.'

'To discuss business?' Charlotte asked, and watched his jaw tighten. 'Because if that was the case then a phone call would have sufficed—flowers and a second-hand apology weren't necessary.'

'Second-hand?'

'They spelt Zander with an X. Anyway it's irrelevant. I have nothing to discuss with you unless it's about business.' Zander was not used to being stood up or turned down and certainly not when he'd deigned to send flowers.

'I wish to talk.'

'You really think that you can just walk in anywhere and get whatever you want?'

'Of course.'

'You're just a spoiled rich boy…'

And he looked to where she stood and knew he could correct her, could tell her there had been nothing spoiled about his childhood, that the privileged life he led now had been built by his hands, but he spoke of his past with no one, although he had, occasionally, with her.

'You don't know anything about my life.'

'I thought I was starting to,' Charlotte said. 'I thought when we walked on that beach, when we went out to dinner, when you took me to bed…'

He was not here to discuss his past; he was here to find out about her, to put to rest the rare guilt she had generated in him, a feeling that did not sit well with him. 'What you said about your mother, about her having to go into a home…'

'I shouldn't have.' Charlotte's response was instant, that precious time in the spa allowing her to speak with clarity, on that subject at least. 'My problems are my own and they have nothing to do with what happened between us, so you can leave now.' She went to open the door, but Zander was not going anywhere.

'I want to know what is happening.'

'I don't want to discuss my mother, and I have nothing to say to you.'

For the first time with a woman he could not leave it there, did not want to leave it there—for although their day had been engineered, although their night had started with cruel intent, it had concluded differently, and he wanted her back. He wanted the Charlotte that had spoken with him, but her stance was closed, her face a mask, and he fought with the one thing he had left.

'What if I *am* here about business?' Zander said.

'Then I'll schedule you an appointment. '

'I have already been more than patient…'

'Really!'

'Do you know how valuable my time is? Instead, you keep me waiting in a restaurant. You will come out with me. I have arranged to take out the yacht. I am considering releasing the land…'

'I just need your signature.' Charlotte did her level best to keep her voice even. 'It isn't necessary to go out on your yacht.'

'Necessary for whom?' came his snobbish response. 'It is how I conduct business.' He paused for a moment. 'Okay, ring Nico and tell him to join me.'

'That's not possible now. I could speak with Paulo.'

'I have no time for him. It is to be Nico or you. We would go out on the boat, then naturally we would share a long lunch, we would talk, and then I would, *perhaps*, sign. In fact…' She could feel her nails digging into her palms as cruelly he continued. 'It should be Nico taking me out, given how much he wants this deal. Perhaps he is not so keen after all. Perhaps given his PA can only spare me a few minutes of her time…'

'You know that is not the case.'

'So where is he?' Zander pushed and of course she could not answer, knew that he had her trapped, and she did not want to be on a boat with him. She just wanted it over and done with, wanted him out of her life.

'You know you don't need to take me out for a signature.'

'I want to, though.'

'You think I'll change my mind, that you'll seduce me again…' The trouble was that he would, he absolutely would, and that was what most terrified her.

'I came here to do business,' Zander said coolly. 'I expect either Nico or yourself on the jetty at midday.' He looked at where she clutched her dressing gown to herself. 'Hopefully you will dress suitably. Speak with Ethina in the boutique, I will tell her to expect you.'

Bastard.

'Nico…' She apologised for disturbing him, but she would not make a move without telling him, and Nico listened as she explained what his brother had in store for her.

'I've told you, you don't have to go out on his yacht with him. I would never ask you to do that.'

'I'm willing to, though. I just want these papers signed, Nico. And then, I'm sorry, I just want to go home.' She took a deep breath for there was so little to lose now. 'I'm having some health issues with my mother and I really need to fly home first thing tomorrow.'

'I'm sorry to hear that. Is there anything I can do to help?'

'I don't know…' she admitted. 'I need to see how she is before I make any decisions.'

'You can cope?' Nico checked. 'With Zander?'

'Of course.'

'Charlotte…'

'I'm working for you, Nico,' she said, because she was, and, yes, she could cope.

If Zander thought she would succumb again to his charms, that a few hours in close confinement on his yacht with him would somehow dissipate the hurt, would have her falling into his bed again, he was wrong.

So wrong, Charlotte thought, and a small smile spread across her lips.

A smile that became more devilish.

A smile that, as she looked in the mirror, reminded her of the old Charlotte. Apart from her work clothes she was so behind with fashion these days, what heaven it would be to update. How wonderful to keep her head with Zander and look brilliant while doing so.

She stood in the boutique, facing a full-length mirror. Ethina, the owner, was far from gushing, was critical. Clearly it was Zander that Ethina had to impress, and, from the purse to her lips as she ran her eyes over Charlotte, she had her work cut out. She had to transform the lily-white body that hadn't so much as set foot in a gym into the groomed beauty expected by the wallet the boutique was attached to.

How many clothes did a signature from a billionaire require?

'Too harsh.' Ethina held a blood-red bikini up to Charlotte's shoulder and then a jade one and then white. Had her mind not been made up as to her course of action, Charlotte would have run out of the exclusive boutique rather than take the shame.

No doubt that was what Zander was expecting.

For her to make do with what was in her case or to grab the first offering Ethina held up. Instead, she stood there and fought down the shame. She listened and watched and slowly, very slowly, marvelled at the skill of the snooty Ethina.

She learnt that the dull silvery-gold string bikini that looked so tacky on the rack looked sensational on her, that it did not clash with the paleness of her skin and that it blended in with the gold of her hair.

'With the right sunglasses...' Ethina continued, 'the right sandals...' There were beautifully cut shorts and cool linen shirts and then for the first time since her project had entered there was a smile on Ethina's face as she eyed Charlotte in the mirror. 'My work is done.'

Even a bag was purchased for her and Ethina said that she would pack it. Charlotte was led to the salon, the oils washed out and her hair brushed, straightened and then curled, all to create one, oh, so casual ponytail, and she felt casual and elegant and possibly a little bit beautiful as she picked up her new bag and headed to the jetty.

Yes, she felt ready to face him.

Zander watched her walk along the jetty.

Saw her ponytail swishing in the breeze. He had expected hesitation, for her to stop and fiddle, to find a mirror, but it was a confident Charlotte who walked towards the boat—and she looked stunning, even with those gorgeous eyes shielded.

She did her best not to sulk.

Instead, she played the game and accepted champagne and the delicacies on offer, laughed at his comments, spoke with him—but not for a second was she herself, and he missed her, he craved her, he wanted her back.

'That is Lathira…' he pointed to the island in the distance '…where Nico grew up.'

'Oh.'

'You know that,' Zander said. 'It was the wealthier of the islands then.' She examined a manicured nail instead of commenting. She was at work, Charlotte reminded herself, there to gather information for Nico. There to confuse Zander with her confidence, there to reclaim some pride.

'And you grew up on Xanos,' Charlotte said. 'What about…?' She swallowed, for she felt like a spy. 'What about your parents?'

'What did he ask you to find out?' Worse than a spy, she felt like a double agent.

'I was just making conversation.'

'You blush when you lie,' Zander said. 'Not a lot, but your neck goes pink.'

They dropped anchor and she didn't feel so brave any more, but tried not to show it.

He took off his shirt and she yearned to do the same, to feel the breeze on her shoulders, but her body thrummed in his presence and it was safer covered. He smiled as she sat on the bench, trying to look detached, trying to ignore the scent of him as he leant over to pick up the sun lotion.

'Could you do my back?' He asked as if he were innocent, as if that olive skin could possibly burn, as if a man like Zander Kargas could possibly feel pain if it did.

'Of course.'

She was stronger than she even knew she was capable of being. Charlotte picked up the tube and imagined it was the vitamin E cream with which she daily oiled her mum. She refused to remember the sheen of his back when it had slid beneath her fingers, refused to notice the ripple of muscles, or to even acknowledge the faint scratches that her nails had made the other night.

'Done!' She even managed a gentle, sisterly slap on his back before she replaced the lid on the tube and felt the teeniest surge of triumph as, without words, she told him he wasn't quite as irresistible as he'd thought. 'How long will we be out for?'

'That depends.'

'On what?' For the first time her anger bubbled to the surface and she fought to check it. Did he think all this would erase the hurt, that a day trip on his luxury yacht would blind her to all he had done?

'I want to talk.'

'We are talking.'

'I want to talk like before.'

'I trusted you then,' Charlotte said.

She did not trust him now.

Did not trust the man who stripped off his shorts and stood before her.

'Time for a swim.' Black eyes met hers. 'Join me?'

'I'd rather not.'

What a lie. Her body was on fire and she wanted to be in the water. Only as he dived off the side did she venture a look from behind her dark glasses, saw the arms that had once held her slice through the water as easily as he had sliced her heart, yet she wanted to be in there with him, wanted the cool of the water, wanted so badly to join him.

Instead, she sat and the linen of her shirt felt like a horse blanket around her shoulders, so she finally allowed herself to take it off. He came back to the boat, dripping and cool and irritated now, for she spoke about the water and the view. She chatted but did not engage in the way they once had.

'We could sunbake,' he offered, 'go further out to the islands.'

'Whatever you want.'

'What do you want?' Zander demanded. 'What amuses Charlotte?'

Clearly nothing did.

'What will it take for you to enjoy it? What do I have to do to—?'

'There's nothing you can do,' she cut in, for did he really think she was so shallow, that a trip on his yacht and champagne could soothe the hurt? 'How can I ever enjoy time with you when I know what you did to me, when I know what you are capable of?'

'I have apologized,' Zander said. He did so rarely, but it had always worked in the past.

'But it still happened,' Charlotte said, and such was the visible regret in his dark eyes, she almost believed it was real. She felt the spell that he cast so easily start to work its charm and she flailed for something else, an antidote to the magic he made, and she found it. 'I know how you treated me, and I know how you treat others, how you do business, the lengths you will go to...' It felt good to say it, easier to be angry on other's behalf, for around him, for herself, she was weak. 'Look what you've done to Xanos.'

'It needed it,' Zander said. 'The place was falling apart, people were leaving in droves. Now it is prosperous.'

'For you, perhaps,' Charlotte said.

'It was a dwindling fishing village, now there are jobs, now the island is thriving.'

'There are no jobs for the locals, though.' She challenged him. 'Except for the taverna that feeds *your* labourers, all the other workers are from the mainland.' He heard her words and he moved to defend himself, to correct her, but there it was again, this guilt that seemed to invade at times when she was around. She was such a wisp of a thing, Zander thought, but she was stronger than most; not in her slender arms that stretched out, exasperated, and not in her voice, which could so easily be drowned by his, but in her resolve, in her beliefs, in her convictions, and he was silenced. 'Will you take me back now?'

'If that is what you want. But I brought you here to find out why, because of me, your mother needs to go in a home.' This time there was no derision in his voice. 'Charlotte, I need to know. I need to put that right at least.'

'Please,' Charlotte said, 'just leave it.'

'I cannot. If Nico is going to fire you because of what happened… I have told you, there is a job for you.'

'A paid mistress?' Charlotte sneered. 'I'm not even going to respond to that offer.'

'I don't understand how your mother—'

'Zander, stop!' Her voice was shrill and she tamed it. 'I'm sorry that I said that.'

'Sorry?' He could not make out this woman, was used to women pouring out their hearts rather than holding back.

'My mother is sick, she has Alzheimer's, and I've been looking after her at home. I don't have the party life that I told you I did. That life was a long time ago.' And she waited, waited for horror to cloud his features, for him to recoil, but still he stood there. 'I lied to you.' She spelt it out and *still* he stood there.

An angel had not been required, but she was close to it now. This was the woman he had thought sleeping with his brother, the party girl he had assumed could handle all he heaped on her. And he knew then how badly he had hurt her, that the heart he had broken this time had been a fragile one.

'Why?'

'I lied to you because…' She screwed her face up in

frustration. 'Because you didn't need to hear it, because it could never impact on you.'

It just had, though.

'I thought I could handle a fling,' Charlotte said simply. 'In fact, I'm quite sure I could have. I just never anticipated that you'd cause me so much pain.' She was terribly honest. 'I'm sorry that I blamed you about my mother, it just felt easier.'

'Easier?'

'I'm starting to sound like her.' She did not need to explain herself to him, Charlotte realised, she just needed to explain it to herself. 'You actually did me a favour...' She gave a wry smile. 'You learn a lot about yourself when difficult times hit.'

'So what did you learn?'

He was the man she'd first met, the man who made her unbend, the man she could talk to, but she was far more wary now. Still, it was a relief to voice what had been whirring in her head.

'That I'm starting to sound like her.' Charlotte explained. 'Bitter, a victim, berating—it was never my intention. She begged me not to put her in a home when she was first diagnosed, told me over and over that I was all she had, that she had done so much for me. I love my mum. Whatever decision I make it's going to hurt. But when I heard myself blaming you, when I used my mum as an excuse...'

'What do you want, Charlotte?'

'I want my life back.' There, she'd said it out loud. 'To go back to flying...'

'No. I don't want to be away all the time while I've still got Mum. Hopefully I'll keep my job and be able to visit Mum a lot.' She was talking as if it were a done deal, but she felt sick inside and she looked beyond the boat to the ocean, wished for a glimpse of peace, but it did not come from the view; instead, it came from a most unexpected source. He put his hand on her shoulder and for the first time her body did not respond to his with a leap of awareness. As his fingers rested on her shoulder, it was a caress that soothed, a caress she wanted to sink into, his voice somehow the one that calmed her.

'I can only imagine what you think of me, and I know my opinion might not mean much to you, but for what it's worth, I think you have made the right choice.'

And his opinion should not matter, except it did, and to hear him approve of her wretched decision brought a sting of relieved tears to her eyes.

'It's a horrible choice, though.'

'There isn't a nice one,' Zander pointed out. 'From impossible situations you make impossible choices. Maybe if your mother had her time again, if she knew how bad it would get, maybe she would be saying the same thing.'

'I doubt it!' Her smile was small but genuine. 'I love her dearly, but she really was the most difficult woman.'

'She probably did her best,' Zander offered, and Charlotte could tell he immediately wished that he hadn't because as her eyes jerked to his, he looked away. She knew he was going to change the subject.

'Maybe yours did, too.'

He stood, did not even attempt a response. 'Do you want to swim? Or we could head back…'

'No.'

He was the one resisting now, he was the one who wanted the safety of shore, and she wanted him to stop, wanted him to talk. 'Maybe she did do her best, Zander.'

'By selling one child and deserting the other?' Zander asked. 'She destroyed my father by leaving. He was a good man, an honourable man, till she left him.' He stopped but only because she put up her hand.

'Please, don't…' Her hand was shaking. She so badly wanted to know what had happened, but she had forgotten the reason was here, did not want him to confide in her when she would have to betray him. She could not reveal that to him, but Zander was one step ahead of her.

'You have to tell Nico what I say to you?'

'How do you know?'

'Rare, the woman who doesn't want to talk about feelings.' She looked up and was surprised to see him smiling. 'That's usually all they want to talk about. Tell him what you must, Charlotte, it makes no difference to me.'

'Why won't you talk to him?'

'There's nothing I want to discuss.'

'He's your twin,' Charlotte said. 'How can you not want to get to know him? How can you not want to find your mum?'

'Because neither of them interest me,' Zander said.

'I'll sign the papers, though—if it helps you.' Which was the reason she was there, yet all she felt was sad.

'If I were Nico…' she started, and then stopped, for Zander's signature was the reason she was there and she had it in her grasp now.

'Go on.'

She dared to go on, dared to speak her truth, whatever the eventual cost. 'I wouldn't want the land. I'd move as far away as I could.' She looked at the most beautiful man she had ever seen, a man who was capable of so very much but was determined to stay locked in hate. 'I don't know why Nico wants to prolong the agony. Why he doesn't just cut his losses…' She stopped talking then, because she understood why. For surely Nico loved him, wanted, however painful, contact with him, wanted the hope that things might one day change.

'You need oil.' He picked up the bottle and changed the subject, gave her the benefit of that beautiful smile that was, she had found out, just a small part of him. 'Your shoulders are burning.'

'Don't try and seduce me, Zander.' She must not give into him, must not just bend to his will. 'I'm not sleeping with you.'

'I just want to oil you.'

'Please.' She shrank away, for she knew what his touch could do. 'What do you want from me, Zander?'

And always Zander surprised her for, as he unstoppered the bottle, as he poured oil on her shoulders, he told her he wanted more than her body as he put in his bid. 'I am leaving Xanos tonight—and I want you to come with me.'

CHAPTER TEN

HER arms were rigid beside her when she felt the sliver of oil touch her skin.

He traced it across her shoulders; she felt first his fingers then his palms and felt as if she was being gently kneaded, moulded. She attempted to retain her self-possession.

'You want me to come with you?'

'Now I know your circumstances, now that I know the truth, we could come to some arrangement that suits.'

'That suits?' Her heart seemed to plummet from the dizzy heights it had soared to, and she berated herself for daring to dream, for considering for a foolish moment that he might purely want her.

'Relax, all I am doing is oiling you.'

'I don't trust you,' she said, for it was true. Neither did her body trust what it might do, for her legs were shaking so much she had to push down her feet to stop them.

'Lie down,' Zander said, removing her sunglasses, and she wished he hadn't for she felt braver behind them.

'I'll do your back.' And as she tensed in resistance, he gave her his word. 'We will not sleep together again till you trust me,' Zander said. 'And you will.'

I won't, her mind insisted, but he lowered the bars of resistance with velvet-cloaked words and she lay on her stomach and felt the oil drizzle on her back and then the bliss of his fingers.

'Come with me.'

'Where?' His hands were on her rib cage now, stroking in the oil.

'Anywhere,' Zander said. 'Away from Nico. I will take care of you. Whatever he pays you—'

'You mean you'll employ me?' She could feel the tears in her eyes and she squeezed them closed.

'Turn over,' he said, and she wanted to see him, she wanted to see him properly so she could understand what he was saying, so she did as he asked.

'I'm not asking you to work for me.' He poured oil to her stomach, but not once did his fingers edge towards gold. 'Just that you do not work for him. I will look after you.'

'Financially?' She pushed his hands away, but they were quickly back and she wanted to sob because they changed her, they made the wrong so very right, made all things possible as now they moved to her waist. She wanted him to tear off her bikini and cool her with his mouth. 'You mean that you'll pay me to be there for you. There's another word for that, Zander.'

And he was so loathsome because all he did was smile. He looked at her tears, her anger, and still all he did was smile, because what abhorred her was completely fine with him.

'If you're looking for my heart, I warn you,' he said, 'I have no heart to give.'

'Then I don't want you.'

'Liar.'

'I don't,' she said, except his hands were at her neck, unfastening the top of her bikini and then moving behind and working the tiny clasp, and so small were her breasts that they barely moved, but she felt sick with excitement and shame. He stared down at them, and she saw the lust in his eyes, the decadent lick of his lips.

'I can't...'

'Can't or won't?' His hands crept to her breasts,

'Can't.' She shuddered, her eyes flashing to his, telling him her truth in the hope it would repel. 'I've told you that I lied. I'm not what you think, I'm not able to travel. It nearly killed me to get away this time.'

'Because of your mother.'

'Yes,' she wept, because the truth should halt his hands, that she was not all she had said she was should have him pause, but his hands moved lower.

'How about a job with no work hours?' She frowned up at him. 'I don't need another PA, Charlotte.'

'I don't want to be kept.'

'Why?' he asked. 'When you'd get the best bits.' He was more tempting than the devil. She could see the best bits, the thick outline of them in his wet bathers. The lull of the boat beneath her back, the sun on her arms, the cool shade of his body shielding her torso did nothing to cool her.

Was it wrong, to want only the best bits?

Wrong to lie there as he eased her bikini bottoms down, to envisage a future as the occasional lover of Zander?

To go back to her life and not worry about bills?

To look after her mother and know she had this as an occasional reward?

She lay naked beneath him and he was so unabashed by her nakedness, so delighted by her, and wicked too, for he picked up the oil and squeezed it where her thighs were clamped closed, like her mind, trying to keep delicious prospects out, trying not to be seduced again by all Zander Kargas offered.

Except his fingers slid in, welcome if uninvited, and she kept her thighs closed but that offered no deterrent. She bit on her lip as he watched her, and she opened her eyes to the beauty of him and could not say no, did not want to say no, so she said nothing, her silence her consent.

He bought her to orgasm so easily.

Too easily almost. It made her feel ashamed, the kettle he could flick on at whim, not that a man like Zander had any need for a kettle. She wanted it all, even if it was impossible. She could not be at his bidding, for her sanity's sake.

'No.' Her hand was reaching out for him, for the supposed best bit, but she pulled it back for she wanted more, wanted the man that came with it, wanted his heart.

'You don't know me.' She thought of her life back home.

'I don't need to.'

And it was cruel but it was his truth.

She could play dress-up once maybe twice a month, escape to a fabulous hotel.

Inhabit a small corner of his life.

And it would be beyond cruel, Charlotte realised.

He did not offer escape. Instead, Zander offered prison, for she would be locked for ever with feelings she could not release. That was what held her hand back.

That made her say no.

'I can't.' She was completely honest. 'I want more than that.'

'There can be no more.'

'There has to be.'

'I don't understand what you want.' He was brutally honest. 'We have known each other one weekend. Isn't it a bit soon to be demanding for ever?'

'That's not what I'm saying.'

'What, then? I am offering you a chance for us to get to know each other better and to remove from you the division of loyalty you have working for Nico. I don't give out rings, Charlotte. I'm offering you now all I will ever give.' He made it completely clear, and she could only admire him for that—he warned her upfront that he would break her heart, and for Charlotte it made the final choice painful but easy.

'Then I choose to live with my head in the clouds. To believe that one day—'

'Someone better than me will come along.' It was his trump card and he played it. He was possibly the only man who could ever play it, for he had driven her to the edge in bed, and to the deepest places in her mind; he was exquisite and beautiful and there could be no better, for her heart had met his on that first phone call and they would forever be joined. He was the best, and it almost killed her to stay strong as he looked down at her naked, flushed body, a body that had just come at his command, and even think there could be someone better.

'He might,' Charlotte said.

'I told you—you blush when you lie. You know there can be no better than what we have.'

'And do you retain exclusive rights?'

'Of course.'

'Do I get the same privilege?' She watched as his tongue rolled in his cheek. She would rather be alone than share him and would go no further with this ridiculous conversation. She was stronger than she'd known, stronger even than Nico, for she could do what his identical twin could not—she could end the painful contact with him, could give up now the hope that things might one day change.

'Can you take me back now, please?'

She stood. Putting on a bikini seemed too complicated with a head that was spinning and hands that were shaking, so she fled down below, pulled on her new clothes from her new bag, and went back to her old heart.

To the one that had the dream that life could one day be different,.

That *he* was somehow waiting.

And clearly it wasn't a dream that Zander shared, for as she sat on a bed she would never sleep in, she heard the engine, felt the movement of the boat as Zander took her back to shore.

Zander spent the hour sailing towards Xanos wrestling with his thoughts.

He sailed the yacht past Lathira, the place his brother had been raised, and then he aimed towards Xanos, to the hell he had hated. Yet it was with new eyes he saw it now.

He saw the beach where he had met her, where they had walked and talked.

He saw the balcony of Ravels where they had kissed and the blackened windows where he had held her.

He saw his island through different eyes, new images made by Charlotte.

He had hurt her, had assumed she could take it, had not recognised her innocence, for he had none himself. He had hurt others too—he had looked at the land he had transformed with no thought to its history, or the people.

The seagulls were loud as the boat neared land, swirling overhead and finally daring to swoop onto the deck, screeching as they squabbled over the remnants of the meal, eating with far more relish than Charlotte had the delicacies he had ordered for her. Still they squawked for more, still, when they should be full, there was hunger, greed that was never satisfied—like his endless quest for a revenge.

For the first time he saw a future that was different, one that did not stink of the past, one that was better, one where he could be with her.

Maybe he did have a heart to give.

Maybe there could be trust.

Someone there for him, someone who did not leave.

He needed to think, he needed the safety of dry land and the solitude of his room before he made the most difficult decision of his life. Then she came up to the deck in shorts and a T-shirt, her hair down and her eyes shielded by glasses again.

'It was a lovely offer, but completely impossible, even if you did give out rings. You don't know my life…'

He wanted to, though.

For the first time he wanted someone in a way he never had. He wanted to know her, about her, to be there for her, to accept the baggage that came with her, instead of hurling it back to defend a black heart.

The sun must have been too strong, he thought. The sky was orange and he wanted it black. He wanted a safe, dark world that was bitter, but he was tired of strangers on his pillow.

'Here.' He handed her the signed contract of sale for the land that Nico wanted. He could not read her expression behind her dark glasses, but from the shake of her hand when he spoke, he guessed that she understood, for with his signature she was no longer obliged to see him for Nico's sake.

'Meet me.' He wanted her now, but he made himself wait. Till he was sure, till he had talked himself out of it perhaps...

Till the time was right.

'Ring Nico when we get back. Tell him you have my signature.' Then he looked at her and he tried for haughty, for assuming, for the arrogance that usually dripped from each word, but instead his eyes implored. 'Meet me tonight, not on behalf of Nico. Hear what I have to say.' And he turned his back to her, for more than anything he hated weakness. 'Meet me for dinner.'

He was a skilled seducer, Charlotte reminded herself. He had said, and would again, anything to get her to his bed.

It was hard to remember the hurt, though, when there was something else in his eyes.

'I don't know.' She was truly scared, not of him but of how he made her feel, how easily she believed in him when she had sworn that she never would again.

'Please be there.'

'If I'm not?'

'Then I'll know,' Zander said, and he took off her glasses and looked deep into her eyes. 'Do we say good-bye here?'

He was choosing to kiss her, Charlotte realised.

He chose to pull her into him to serve as a constant reminder. He kissed her better than the first time and maybe for the last time; he kissed her with his mouth and she felt it with her heart. 'Please...' He dropped contact for he had to think, but once he had done that, everything would change.

Change can be good, Zander thought as he looked into the blue that could perhaps forever entrance him.

The same can be good too, Zander mused as he thought of her head on the pillow beside him from this night for ever. 'Meet me tonight.'

CHAPTER ELEVEN

HE WENT to his suite and waited for sense to return.

He downed a drink as if were medicine, felt the burn in his gut and waited for normal services to resume, for him to remember how much she annoyed him. Except he could recall not an instant, not a laugh that had irritated him, or questions that had irked. For the first time he had wanted to tell all to another. Still, he racked his brains to find fault somehow, to prove himself right, to tell himself that this could not work, that he was mad to consider a future with her.

But consider it he did.

So too did she.

Had there been love in those coal-black eyes—was there more that he might be prepared to give?

It wasn't the yacht or the trappings that lured her, it was the voice that had filled her grey bedroom those mornings that she wanted to hear for ever; it was the man who had made her smile and melt. She wanted so much more of him.

She blasted her body and face with the shower, told

herself not to get her hopes up, that this was a man who had hurt her deeply, a man who had shamed her badly. Logic told her that this was a man she should not trust.

The phone rang and it was Nico. She had to remember where, for now at least, her duties lay. She would enjoy giving him the good news about the land. But instead of Nico it was Constantine with sad news.

'He passed away,' Constantine said. 'Nico's father passed away a couple of hours ago. In the end it was peaceful and they made their peace, which is good.'

Charlotte offered her condolences and then told Constantine to pass on that she had Zander's signature, but they both knew it was not really the land that Nico wanted but the brother and the mother and the history that came with it.

'Charlotte, you know we have tried all the homes and hostels on Xanos and Lathira but the nurses here were talking and there is one we have missed. It's in the nunnery in the northern hills of Xanos, they take in a few fallen women and care for them. I have rung and spoken to them and I think I might have found her. Please, Charlotte, can you go and find out? I don't want to tell Nico until I am certain. Can you go now?'

'Of course.' Charlotte looked at the clock. She could surely do it. If she was a bit late for dinner, Zander would have to understand.

It wasn't just for Nico that she said yes, neither was it for duty. She wanted to face Zander tonight with the truth on the table. As she walked through the foyer, past the various boutiques, she glanced at the jeweller's, at an empty space where the necklace had been, and she actually held hope.

She was sure, completely sure, that she was doing the right thing by him, that it was the truth that was needed here.

And she was almost sure that Zander wasn't about to break her heart again.

The driver was delighted by the blonde passenger who spoke a little Greek, but Charlotte barely replied to his questions as the car threaded its way along the hillside and came to rest at the nunnery.

There was no reception on her mobile phone, so she asked the driver to wait and stalled his protests with cash. Then she rang the bell and, when it was answered, she was welcomed into the old building. She spoke for a while with two kindly nuns, one of whom spoke a little English, which helped when Charlotte's Greek was not up to the job.

'She speaks of the twins all the time,' the nun explained. 'She has two plastic dolls that she holds and will not let go of. It is sad...'

'Can I see her?' Even now she dared not get her hopes up, for she had thought she was close to finding her so many times before.

'Of course. If she can see her sons, or even know that they are okay, maybe she can go to God in peace.'

'She's only young, though,' Charlotte said, for the woman they were speaking about was only around fifty, she had been told.

'She has lived a hard life.'

It was impossible to remember she was supposed to be working as she walked into the sparsely furnished room for as she walked over to Roula, it was Zander who was in her heart.

It *was* Roula. She could now, without hearing a word from the woman, ring Nico and tell him his mother had been found, for the eyes that stared into the distance had been passed on to her sons, the pain in them too. Charlotte wanted to embrace her, but instead she approached slowly.

'This is Charlotte,' the nun explained to a vacant-looking face of Roula. 'She works for Nico...' The old lady's eyes jerked to hers.

'He has been looking for you,' Charlotte said in Greek.

'Alexandros?' Roula begged, and Charlotte could not lie to her. Neither could she stand to tell her the truth, that the son she longed for hated her.

'I know Zander too,' she settled for and then, with Charlotte's sparse Greek and the nun's sparse English, they sat, slowly piecing together her story. Though she was supposed to be meeting Zander, Charlotte knew this was more important. She listened to the woman as her agony was slowly revealed. There was no question of rushing her, no impulse to ring Nico, no thought to the fading light outside or the taxi driver waiting, no thought even of Zander sitting waiting for her at a dinner table. Time did not matter for the moment, for these were words that Zander needed to hear.

CHAPTER TWELVE

'TONIGHT *they have their own rooms,' Alexandros said. 'Separate rooms.'*

'What harm...?' Roula started and then stopped. She had learnt not to question Alexandros's decisions, but on this one she had to stand up to him. It would be cruel to separate the babies, so she tried another route. 'They will wake you with their tears.'

'Let them cry—that is the way they will learn that at night you are with me.' He ran a hand between her thighs, told her that tonight there would be no excuses— not that he listened when she made them.

Her only relief was the slam of the door when he left to spend the day sitting outside the taverna, play- ing cards and drinking, but Roula's relief lasted just a moment before the countdown started, dreading his re- turn.

Seventeen and the mother of twins, they were her only shining light. More beautiful than any other babies, she could watch them sleep for hours, the little snubs of their noses pushed up by their fingers as they sucked on their thumbs, eyelashes so long that they met the curve

*of their cheeks. Sometimes one would open his eyes to
the other. Huge black eyes would gaze at his brother,
soothed by what he saw, and then close again.*

*Mirror-image twins, the midwife had told Roula when
she had delivered them. Identical, but opposite, one
right-handed the other left. Their soft baby hair swirled
to the right on Nico, to the left on little Alexandros.*

*At almost a year, they still shared a cot, screaming
if she tried to separate them. Even if their cribs were
pushed together their protests would not abate. Now he
would force them into separate rooms.*

*And she would hear their screams all night as her
husband used her body, and Roula could not take it any
more.*

Would not.

*Her father would surely help if he knew. Alexandros
did not like her to go out so she had seen her father only
a couple of times since her marriage—he had wanted
her to marry as the little money he got for his paintings
could not support them both. He had been a little eccen-
tric since her mother's death; he preferred to be alone.
But he would surely not want this life for his daughter
and grandsons.*

*'Now,' she told herself. 'You must do it now.' She
had maybe five or six hours before Alexandros returned. She ran down the hallway, pulled out a case
and filled it with the few clothes she had for her babies,
and then she ran into the kitchen to a jar she had hidden, filled with money she had been secretly hoarding
for months now.*

'This is how you repay me?' Roula froze when she heard his voice, and then simply detached herself as he beat her, as he told her she was a thief to take from the man who put a roof over her head. 'You want to leave, then get out!' How her heart soared for a brief moment, but then Alexandros dealt his most brutal blow. 'You get half...' He hauled her to the bedroom where her babies lay screaming, woken by the terrible sounds. 'Which one is the firstborn?' He did not recognise his own sons. 'Which one is Alexandros?'

When she answered he picked up the other babe and thrust Nico at her.

'Take him, and get out.'

She ran to her father's, clutching Nico. She was terrified for Alexandros left alone with him, sure that her father would help her sort it out. Along the streets she ran till finally home was in view, except it was boarded up. Her father was now dead, the disgusted neighbours told her, for she had neglected him in his final days and had not bothered to attend his funeral. The worst was finding out that her husband had been informed, had known, and not thought to tell her.

'We will get your brother back,' she said to a screaming Nico. The local policeman drank regularly with Alexandros so he would be no help, but she would go to the main town of Xanos, which was on the north of the island, to the lawyer that was there.

She took a ride on a truck and had to pay the driver in the vilest of ways, but she did it for her son, and she *did it many times again when she found that the rich young lawyer wanted money up front before helping her.*

A little cheap ouzo from the lid meant Nico slept at night and she could earn more money. The rest of the bottle got her through.

And she tried.

Till one day, sitting holding her baby in an alleyway, she heard a man's voice.

'How much?'

Roula looked up and she was about to name her paltry fee, but there was a woman standing next to him, and that was one thing Roula would not do.

'I'm not interested.'

Except he did not want her body. 'How much for him?'

He told her they were childless, that they were on holiday from the mainland to get over their grief. He told her about the money and education they could give her beautiful boy, that they would move to the neighboring island of Lathira and would raise him as their own. She thought of Alexandros, who was still with that monster, and somehow she had to save him. She thought of the ouzo and the clients she would service tonight and all the terrible things she had done. Surely Nico deserved better.

He wailed in protest as the stranger's wife lifted him. Just as he had those first awful nights when he had missed little Alexandros so badly. But he would settle, Roula told herself as finally she sat in the lawyer's wait-

ing room and signed over one son in the hope of saving the other.

Nico would settle, Roula told herself again as the couple left with her baby. Soon Nico would forget.

She, on the other hand, would spend the rest of her life trying to.

CHAPTER THIRTEEN

'ZANDER…'

As soon as she had phone reception, she called Zander, though she should have called Nico first.

'I'm sorry I couldn't get there in time… I'm on my way now.'

'Are you okay?' She heard his immediate concern. 'You sound as if you have been crying.' Only in the taxi had she broken down, but she tried to disguise it from Zander, for surely it was not her place to weep about this to him.

'I'm okay. I should be there in an hour.'

The reception was terrible and Zander commented on it. 'Where are you?'

'I'm in the hills.'

'The hills? I thought you were meeting me.'

'I'm in a taxi and I'm on my way. Nico asked me…' She faltered, for the mention of Nico's name seemed to light a flare. 'I had something to do for Nico.'

'Something so important that you leave me waiting. You have my signature already, which was what he wanted.'

She looked to her watch. It was long after eight and though she *must* tell Nico first, it was Zander she loved. 'Nico had a lead on your mother that he asked me to follow up. Zander, I've found her. I've just come from speaking with your mother.'

And all she heard was the click of the phone and for a moment thought he had lost the signal, but when she rang again and he didn't answer, when she tried once more and it just rang, she knew he was leaving, knew that in his eyes it had happened again—that she had chosen against him.

She must ring Nico, must remember where her duty lay. 'I've found her,' she said when Constantine answered the phone. Unlike Zander, Constantine immediately asked how Roula was. 'She's fragile,' Charlotte said, and told her a little of the story, arranging to meet with them tomorrow, to explain better face to face. 'There's one thing I don't understand, though...' Charlotte frowned as she spoke with Constantine, for there was one thing she wanted to sort out before she spoke with Zander. 'Roula had the money when she sold Nico so why didn't she go back to the lawyer? Why didn't she use the money to try and get to Zander?'

'Because the lawyer kept upping his fees. Because the lawyer did not want to work for Roula and have her exposing all that he had done.'

'How do you know that?' Charlotte asked.

'Because that lawyer was my father.'

There was pain all around, Charlotte realised. A pain that ran so deep, perhaps too deep for healing, but surely if Nico and Constantine could work through it, then she and Zander stood a chance. She spent the rest of the journey pleading with the driver to please go faster and flew out of the taxi before it had even come fully to a halt. Dashing into the foyer, she saw luxurious cases on the gold trolley and almost wept with relief that Zander was still there.

'Zander, please…' She ran up to him as he walked out to the waiting car. 'I'm sorry but Nico—'

'Nico?' He hated that word and this time it showed. This time he spat it out. 'Nico snaps his fingers and you run. You had plans with me and yet you drop them for him.'

'I met your mum!' Charlotte said. 'I spoke with your mum. Don't you even want to know how she is?'

'No.' It was that simple to Zander. 'I care nothing for her. She is a poor excuse for you to use. I asked you to be there tonight, I was going to…' And he could not say it, for he had been a fool to even think it, think for a moment that they could ever be.

'Going to what?' she pushed, because she wanted to know, wanted to believe that love might have been on offer tonight, wanted to remind him of all he was losing.

'Give you this.' He handed her a thick velvet box, but it came with no meaning, for even rubies and diamonds shone dull without love.

'Just this?' Charlotte said, which seemed strange when the necklace was worth a small mortgage, but she was sure, so sure there had been more to come.

'What else were you expecting?' He frowned. 'Oh, and by the way, I've reconsidered the job offer.'

'Job offer?'

'We discussed you working for me?' He twisted the knife. 'I prefer someone a little more reliable—someone who does not dash off when we have plans. Still…' he gave a tight shrug '…we have had some pleasant times.' He glanced at the box. 'Have it.'

'For services rendered?'

'Don't be crass.'

'That's how you just made me feel.' And there was nothing left to dream, for it had always been impossible. 'I'd say no anyway.' She looked at the stone of his face, at eyes that refused to warm, at the immutable man that was Zander. 'Even if it was more than a job, even if it was more than your mistress, no matter what you were going to offer, I'd still say no.'

Was that a smirk on his face, yes, it was, and it incensed her.

'I would say no.'

'Liar.' It was the closest he would come to admitting that the night could have been very different, that had she not chosen Nico, he would have offered it all.

'Of course I would. You've got a mother who loves you. You don't know what happened, you don't know what she went through…'

'She's had thirty years to come up with her excuses. Whatever she told you—'

'It's nothing to do with what your mother told me,' Charlotte interrupted. 'It's to do with you, Zander.

You've got a whole family waiting, a whole parade of people who want to get to know you, and all you choose is pain. I would say no to whatever you offer, for it would be like living with my mother—and I've done my time with bitter.' And then she looked straight at him. 'It would be worse, in fact. My mother has genuinely forgotten her past, whereas you choose not to know. Your brother is grieving tonight but your black heart cares nothing for that.'

'Nico has what he wants from me—he has the land. Tell him I am selling Xanos. Run to your boss with that bit of information and see if he pays you a bonus for giving him the heads up.'

'It isn't Xanos Nico wants!' Charlotte said pleadingly. 'Can't you see that when you hurt Nico, you hurt me?' Her words came out wrong, her thoughts too jumbled, but she didn't attempt to explain. 'I know what I want, so thank you for helping me see it. I know what I want now.' She held out the box but he did not take it. Neither did he ask her to explain what it was she wanted, but she told him. She looked at him, and he did not flinch as she said it, but she watched his face turn grey, watched his jaw clench just a fraction.

'I want what your brother's got.'

She moved her lips closer to his ear and could have sworn she heard the thud of his black heart as she spoke on. 'I want everything your brother has—a home, babies, love, acceptance and forgiveness, all the things that you can never give.' How cruelly she taunted him, but better that than not say it, better that than he never see. 'I want what Nico has.'

'Well, you've made the right choice,' Zander responded, 'because you'll never get it from me.'

He climbed into a car that would take him the short distance to the jetty, and she stood watching the seaplane lift into the sky and it hurt, for she wanted to be on it, wanted so badly to be with him, but not this way, never this way. She walked the streets of Xanos that night and wandered down to the beach. How she longed to ring him, but knew she must not.

She felt rain start to fall, winter rain that came from the north and was cold and driving, but as she sat on the beach and shivered, it did not feel like rain. Zander had left, signed over the land, walked out, not just on her but the truth, and it felt as if right now, this minute, he was washing his hands of Xanos.

Cleansing himself of her.

CHAPTER FOURTEEN

HE TRIED.

Every part of him tried to remove Xanos from his heart. For the first time he ordered his team to respond to the expressions of interest in the hotel, the land, the entire development. He wanted it sold, he simply wanted it gone.

Zander wasn't baiting Nico, but it came as no surprise that Nico was a serious bidder. There were few who could afford it, fewer still who had a heart in the place, and of course his brother wanted it.

Nico wanted something else too, something Zander could never give.

'No.' Zander's response to his legal team was instant, for it was all done through them, there had been no conversations between the brothers. 'I'm not interested in a partnership.' He moved to the window, stared out to what was surely the most beautiful harbour in the world, to glimpses of beaches that should, after all this time, feel like home, so why was his heart in Xanos? 'He can buy it all or nothing.'

Why did it hurt as his lawyers made calls, as he shed

a painful past and moved towards his future? Why did it hurt to listen to his lawyer inform Nico's team they would be looking at all offers and get back to them soon.

'She wants to know how soon is soon.' The lawyer put the phone on mute. 'Apparently, Nico Eliades does not want to be kept waiting for your decision as he has been in the past. He has another development he is keen on and will be retracting his offer at the end of the week.'

'Tell Paulo—'

'It's not his lawyer on the line, it's his PA, with a direct message from Eliades.'

It was Nico baiting him this time, Zander realised, for Charlotte was the only thing that had bound them. Were it not for her, he might not even have bothered going to Xanos to confront his brother. It had been the lure of her voice that had changed his plans, had made him go to the island he hated. It had been Charlotte who'd had him stay on those extra days and Nico knew it.

'Tell her…' Zander said, but his voice trailed off, because it was late afternoon in Australia and early morning in London, and he *wanted* her voice and the image of her in bed; he wanted to go back to what they'd had before. Which was impossible of course, and it was impossible too to move forward, for he did not have a heart to give—except it seemed to be beating just now, pounding in his chest and demanding the sound of her voice to soothe it. And there beneath his heart, his soul also demanded, but he shut it down with bile, would not give in to Nico, would not let him use Charlotte as his pawn. 'Give me the phone,' Zander said, but did not ask for privacy, for there were few words to be said. 'My staff will get back to you when I tell them to. Tell your boss that, tell him too that he is the one *using* you, but I don't care who calls, I don't care—'

'I'll pass it on.' The clipped words halted him, the sound of a woman's voice, but not *hers*.

'I thought I was speaking with Eliades's PA.'

'You are.'

He did ask for privacy then, flicked his staff out of his office with a brief wave of his hand, before resuming the conversation. 'I usually deal with Charlotte.'

'Ms Edwards is no longer working for Mr Eliades.'

'Since?'

'I'll pass on your message to Mr Eliades.' Nico's incredibly efficient new PA was not going to waste a moment of her boss's valuable time discussing her predecessor.

It was she who rang off and Zander stood there as he lost that last link to Charlotte. She was away from Nico. It should bring relief.

But relief was absent.

He had looked forward to their calls far more than he should.

He gazed out at the richest view in Australia, felt a chill in his skin beneath his luxurious suit, for he had everything, yet he had nothing.

When you hurt Nico, you hurt me.

It was as if she were in the room with him.

He picked up the phone and rang what had once been

Charlotte's number and, of course, Nico's new PA answered. He knew there was only one way to find out about her. 'Can you arrange a meeting for me?' He would do it only for Charlotte. 'With my brother.'

CHAPTER FIFTEEN

'WHY would you want a partnership?'

Zander had been surprised at the choice of venue, sure they would sit in a meeting room at Ravels or perhaps in an office in Athens, but instead Nico had asked him to come to his home. Zander could taste bile as he walked through the stone arch and up the steps of what had once been his grandfather's house. He had accepted the cool greeting of Nico's wife and now sat, grateful for the drink she offered him, as he asked his brother a question that burned.

'Is that not what brothers do?' Nico answered. 'I do not like the plans you have for the remaining part of the island, but I cannot deny what you have achieved so far—'

'At the expense of the people.'

'You have sorted that,' Nico said. 'You have repaid them. There are locals now working at the hotel, in the shops and bars. Xanos is a happier place now. Why would you want to walk away from it, from all you have achieved?'

'Because...' Zander said, but did not qualify it, did

not tell Nico that achieving prosperity for Xanos had never been his intention. He had wanted it gone, to change the landscape he so hated, as if somehow he could erase the past. But he did not share his thoughts with others, did not confide, well, not usually. He had with Charlotte, but he chose not to go there yet. He wanted to know if Nico had fired her, wanted to know if she was doing okay, and if sitting here meant he found out, he'd do it.

'I am not going to play games. Your offer is fair and I accept it. I will have my staff move things along.' He glanced up at the wall behind Nico, to a picture that looked like a jigsaw, and saw that it was the garden he had just walked through. He could see two babies sitting in the grass and he tore his eyes away, would not ask if it was Nicos himself, would not stand and walk over to examine it more closely, he just would not be drawn in. He wanted Xanos gone, wanted distance, he was here for one thing only. 'I will speak with your PA…' He tried to do it casually, tried to change the subject naturally. 'I note that Charlotte is no longer working for you.'

'That's right.' His brother was far too like him, Zander realized, for he gave nothing away uninvited.

'Did you fire her?'

'My staff are not your concern.'

'I am not asking after your staff.' He felt ridiculously uncomfortable, would have liked to loosen his tie, but refused to. 'I am asking after Charlotte.'

'Her personal situation is not for me to discuss.'

'Is she okay?'

'Perhaps you should ask her.'

'I would, had I her number. I assume it was a work phone?'

'I'll ring her,' Nico offered, 'ask if she is okay with me giving her number to you.'

'Please, don't.' Zander stood. 'I just want to know that everything is okay. I don't want to make contact…'

'Why?'

'Because,' Zander said, and again did not qualify, for how could he confide, how could he say what he was feeling, and who on God's earth would understand?

'Why would you not want to speak with her?'

'Because it was just…' He couldn't even say it, could not relegate it to a one-night stand, so instead he sat in silence and the discomfort became unbearable. There was no relief to be had when Nico changed the subject.

'I spoke with our mother…'

'Good for you,' Zander said, and now he wanted out, he wanted to be gone.

'She had her reasons…'

'She's had many years to get her story straight.' Zander's heart was black and he knew it, far, far too black for the light that was Charlotte. A lifetime of hate must have burnt a hole in his soul and he would not taint her. 'I wish you well.' He went to shake his brother's hand and changed his mind. He could hardly stand to look at him, could hardly stand the sight of him, for it felt as if he were looking at himself—a better self, Zander realised, for again it was his brother who had everything, everything he wanted.

He could hear Constantine in the kitchen, could feel the love that filled the home, everything that must be denied him.

'Do you not want to see your nephew?' Nico asked.

He did not want to see him, did not want to fuss and admire a baby, did not want to see more of what he could never have, but Nico would have none of it. Nico walked along a hallway, clearly expecting Zander to follow him.

He would glance in and then leave, Zander decided.

Perhaps admire the babe and then ask once more after Charlotte, for he so badly needed to know that she was okay.

It was for her that he walked the corridor, for her he walked to the crib but for himself he stood there.

And he must have a soul, for right there beneath his heart it wanted to howl. Right there beneath his heart it seemed to shatter and destabilize the knees beneath it. He stared at the babe, his little nose pushed up by fingers, his eyes opening to find out what the noise was. And the baby did not know the man he was gazing at was not his father. All he saw were familiar black eyes and he smiled as if it was a face that comforted, smiled as if it was he, Zander, who soothed him. Then he closed his eyes and went back to sleep.

Nico knew how his brother felt, for his first real look at his son had been by this very crib. The first time he had looked into his son's eyes he had felt as if he was looking into his own, and he now knew he had been looking into his brother's. He knew Zander was remembering a time that could not logically be remembered, when life had been simple, a time when the sight of the other, a look at yourself, had been all it had taken to feel safe.

When you hurt Nico, you hurt me.

Zander could hear her voice in the room with him again, and more than anything he wished it was true, that at this difficult, agonising moment she was here, for he wanted to turn around and see her.

'This is the age we were parted,' Nico said, and to Zander his voice came from a distance. 'This was the age he made her leave and kept only you—the firstborn.'

'She left and chose you,' Zander corrected. 'The good one, the nice one...'

'No.'

He could not face the truth, could not hear it from his brother, could not believe it, for it changed every piece of the past. He raced from the house with questions unanswered, walked the beach and the streets like a drunk in a rage, for he could not stand to hear it, could not face the music, could not be alone as his pompous, lucky, chosen brother sat in a house that was a home.

So he took the plane to Rhodes, blasted the casino and hated himself more for winning. He drank hundred-year-old brandy and it barely touched sides. He wanted it to be easy, wanted to want, as he had before, the women who flocked to him, but knew tonight, for their sakes, that he was safer to be alone. So he paced the floors of the Imperial Suite, and nothing, not money, not brandy, could sate him; nothing in these luxurious confines could tame or sedate him. He waited for sunrise, for the clarity of a morning that was still a couple of hours away—but the sun did not rise, he remembered, it was we who moved towards it. He thought of that first morning phone call, the difference in time that had brought her to him, thought of her in London deeper in the darkness now than he.

She messed with his head, Zander decided. Charlotte messed with his head and changed things and he paced harder. He wanted to get on the plane and chase endless darkness, not run to the morning and the painful light it would bring. But he was weary from running, exhausted from it, knew he had to face the fact that there was nothing now that he would not do to be with her.

And he paced, for he did not know how to find her, did not know how to move forward without going back, yet he could not stand to go back without her.

Nico paced with him not beside him, but in Xanos, for he had worn the same path recently, knew the pit of despair that his brother was now in. He paced his house and garden through the night. He felt his brother's rage, the hurt and anger, but Nico believed in the pendulum, knew that Zander would calm down. He believed in it so fiercely, was so connected with his brother that night, that he knew the moment Zander made his decision.

'Nico.' He looked up at his wife, saw the concern in her face as she came out to the dark garden—the sound of the fountains audible now, the world coming back into focus as he stepped back from his brother's pain and looked into her eyes. How lucky he had been to have her there when the truth had surfaced, how much cooler she had made the hell he'd plunged into.

'I want to help him,' Nico said, as if it was that simple, as if the man who hated him would want his help. But even if she did not approve of his brother, Constantine was always there for him, with a word, with a smile that soothed.

'Then do.'

CHAPTER SIXTEEN

SHE missed him far more than she should.

Far more than one should miss a man who had caused so much pain, Charlotte reminded herself as she woke to the morning and another day without Zander.

The heating came on, the pipes filling, spreading warmth through the house, and she wished it would do the same for her heart, for Zander's heart too. She lay for a moment with her head in the clouds, imagined that he was near, that things were different, and though she loved visiting dreams, she knew she couldn't linger. She put a toe out to the carpet and then pulled it back in, but she had to get up. There was a nurse coming at nine and she wanted the house a little more ordered before she arrived.

Charlotte hauled herself out of bed. The bedroom was freezing as she walked across it but as she caught sight of herself in the mirror, the reflection was not unfamiliar. She did not see a woman living a life she was not happy with. Instead, she saw herself staring back. She was dressed in faded lemon pyjamas, her hair was in need of a wash, but she was wearing a hundred-thousand-dollar necklace, and she could look into the mirror and smile. The hardest weeks of her life lay ahead, yet somehow she knew she could handle it and was at peace with the choices she had made.

She *was* bound to her mother, Roula had taught her that. Sitting talking to Roula, listening as she'd relived the mistake made long ago, hearing her pain, Charlotte had realised that she was bound to her mother for ever— only not out of duty, but love.

Still, the ringing of the doorbell made her grumble, sure that the nursing agency had messed up the times again. She pulled the door open and then promptly closed it, not in anger, just in shock, for there should surely be a warning alert on a cold winter morning when the man of your dreams comes knocking at your door.

'Charlotte!' He opened the letterbox, which was in line with her crotch, and she jumped to the side.

'Can we talk?'

'Now?'

'Right now.' She heard the need, the plea, felt the urgency, and she opened the door to a man only her heart recognised. She saw the unkempt suit, a jaw that needed a razor and eyes that were bloodshot, and she could smell brandy, but his soul shone bright and she could never not let him in.

'It was not a job I was going to offer you…'

'I know.'

'And I was not going to ask you to be my mistress that night.'

'I know that too.'

'And would you still have said no?'

'No,' Charlotte admitted, for had she made it to dinner, had he offered her his world and an exclusive part in his life, hell, she'd have said yes in a heartbeat, but she was stronger than that now. 'Though I'm sure I'd have lived to regret saying yes.' It was such a hard thing to say. 'I want the Zander I thought I knew, the one I first met. The one who could not wait to meet with his brother...'

'I spoke to Nico. I went to see him yesterday.' Charlotte opened her mouth to speak, knew just how big this was, but she forced herself to say nothing, to let him tell her in his own time. 'He gave me your address, early this morning he texted it to me. I understand if you have little to say to me but I have to know, did I cost you your job?'

'No.' Immediately she shook her head. 'No...I...' She did not want to say it here, did not want to discuss such things in the hall. 'Come through.'

She saw him blink in surprise as she led him not to the lounge but to her bedroom, for it was the only place in the house that was truly hers. She sat on the bed and he perched on the jumble of clothes that hid her chair and she said the hardest words.

'I was going to put Mum in a home. I just couldn't keep looking after her and I had to work and it would have been the right decision at the time. But when I got back I had some bad news about her health—Mum's only got a few months left to live.' She took a big breath because it was so hard to say it, but she forced herself, said it quickly, lightly, even though it masked so much hurt. 'So I've bunged a bit of money on the mortgage and I'm taking a year off from my job.'

'You could have sold the necklace.' He smiled to see it around her neck, smiled that it was not locked up in a box but that she wore it with pyjamas. 'I was trying to take care of you with that.'

'I'd never sell it,' Charlotte said. 'No matter what it's worth, it's worth more than money to me.'

He looked at her face, at the dull eyes and the unwashed hair, and all he could see was Charlotte.

'You could have rung,' she said. 'You should have given me some warning.'

'I wanted to see you.'

'Well, now you have,' Charlotte said. 'And I'm fine. I still have a job when I'm ready to go back. You can leave with your conscience clear.'

But he did not.

'You must be exhausted,' Zander said, as even with a racing heart she stifled a yawn.

'A bit,' she admitted. 'But I just want to finish what I started. I couldn't go on looking after Mum indefinitely, I can see that now, but...' He said nothing, he just looked. 'It isn't indefinite any more and I want to focus on the time we have. I've got a nurse that comes in and we're going on holiday next week.' Charlotte rolled her eyes. 'Don't ask me how we'll manage but I've booked a cottage by the beach and, freezing or not, we're going to walk on the beach and feed the seagulls. Nico's actually been wonderful...' And she watched because this time his face did not darken, neither did he flinch at the mention of his brother, he just looked at her with eyes that were open to her questions now. 'You went to see him?'

'I went to see him to find out about you. When I spoke with his new PA I could not stand it that you had left, that Nico might have fired you...'

'I can go back any time,' Charlotte said, though she doubted she actually could, for it would kill her to see Nico and not Zander; it would be agony to be close to someone just a step away from the man she truly wanted. 'You went to see him just for that?'

He paused and then shook his head. 'No, I also went to find out about me, about him, about our mother.'

'And did you?'

'No.' He had run from the truth, for very deep reasons, but he could not keep running any longer. The truth was waiting and he had somehow to move forward and greet it, and the only way he could do that was with her. 'I would rather hear the truth from you,' Zander said. 'With you.'

'She loved you,' Charlotte said simply. 'She still does.' She watched as he pressed his fingers into his eyes, didn't understand the shake of his head and his unwillingness to believe it, and she told him his story as had been relayed to her through his mother and the nun, but still he denied it, still he refused to believe. 'She didn't choose Nico. Zander, your father gave her no choice in anything. He completely controlled her. She did everything she could to go back for you.'

'No.' Still he was adamant; still he argued that black was white and Charlotte just did not understand. Why would he refuse the antidote to his pain.?

'Why won't you believe her, Zander? Why do you…?' She closed her eyes in frustration, for still he would not be swayed, still he would not take the love that was all around him if only he reached out to it. 'She's sitting in a nursing home, clutching two plastic dolls, desperate to see her sons. It's cruel that you…' She halted herself for she did not want it to be so, did not want Constantine's words to be true, did not want the father-son rule to apply. 'Why can't you just accept…?'

'Because that's not what I *know*.' He did not shout it, but he might as well have. She felt the hairs rise on her neck, felt her body jolt as if he had roared, and Charlotte heard it so loud and so clear that it hurt. 'He fell apart when she left. The drinking and the misery and the hell was all of her making. She did that to him.' She watched as he stopped, as everything he knew dispersed. 'That is what I need to believe, needed to believe to survive. The man I loved…' He halted, for it hurt to admit it, hurt to be five years old and hear the roar of his father's voice, hurt to recall the confusion.

'You loved him?'

'Of course—he was my father,' Zander said, because to a child it was that simple. 'And then later I felt sorry for him, thought I made things worse for him by being there, and then all I did was hate him, for not being strong enough to move on from what she had done.' He looked at Charlotte. 'He told me he was a good man, an honourable man, a hard-working man till she left him. And I believed him, till this very moment I believed him—I had to. All he told me was a lie, and I should have seen it. As if he was ever going to sit down and tell me the truth…'

'She loved you,' Charlotte said. 'She always has.'

'What does that make him, then?' Zander asked. She had thought him blind, thought he had simply chosen pain, but she saw him very differently now. She saw how hard he had tried to remain loyal to the memory of the father that had raised him—a father, that despite it all, he had loved.

'Maybe he was hurting too?' Charlotte offered, but some things were very hard to forgive. 'Perhaps you need to find out more about him.'

And one day he would, Zander decided. One day he would, and he would try to do it without hate in his heart.

'I understand now what you said…' He saw her frown. 'That when I hurt him I hurt you.' Still her frown deepened. 'That Nico is a part of me and when I hurt him, I hurt myself…which hurts you.'

'Actually…' Oh, God, should she tell him she'd just got her words mixed up, that it wasn't some wise saying, just her mouth moving too fast?

'What I meant…' But she stopped talking and smiled instead, saw his exhaustion and wanted to extinguish it. She did not say another word but climbed into bed and closed her eyes.

And he made dreams real, because he undressed and climbed into her single bed, and held her for a moment.

'I have spent my life hating.' He said it to her neck. 'I cannot imagine the outcome had you not come into my life. The day that mattered the most to me, the day I had focused on for so very long, suddenly became less important than the day that came before it, the day I spent with you.'

He kissed her neck and then he said it.

'I love you, Charlotte.'

But she closed her eyes, because it was still impossible. 'This is me,' Charlotte said. 'I can't leave Mum.'

'You don't have to.'

'You say that now…' She was scared to look to the future, scared of the shouts when any moment now her mother awoke, scared of him making a promise that reality would not let him keep. 'When you see how hard it is…'

'Why would I change you?' Zander asked. 'I have never had a proper family. I am told most come with good and bad?'

'They do.'

'I will never hurt the good,' Zander said, 'and I will do my best to ease the bad.'

She could hear the rain against the window and the bus pulling up at the stop outside. His voice was in her ear, as it had been so many times, but this time there was the breath on her ear that meant he was close by.

He had said she must never make love with him till

she trusted him again, and now she handed her heart over willingly, knew it would be safe with him.

He made love for the first time in the morning; that morning they actually made *love*, and it was, as Charlotte told him afterwards as she lay in her bed with him, perfect.

'It would be perfect had I brought a ring,' Zander said. 'However, I was not exactly thinking straight on my way to you.'

'You don't give out rings, remember.' She did not need a ring to know his love.

'Not easily,' Zander said. 'But it is what I want for you. Mrs Kargas.' His name did not hurt now when he said it. With Charlotte bearing it, he could say it proudly.

For their future was together.

EPILOGUE

HE MADE every day a memory.

And not just for Charlotte.

She sat on the beach beside her mother, as she did most late afternoons, stared out at the glorious Mediterranean, and when her mother was starting to get tired, Charlotte would open up the package she had brought, toss out some food and wait for the seagulls. It never failed to make her mother smile, to laugh as she once had, and though Charlotte could not be sure if her mother was going back to earlier times or just smiling at today, every day it was more than worth it.

'Is she ready to go back to the house?' Agira asked, walking over and smiling, a genuine smile that was warm and caring, and Charlotte knew she was blessed to have Agira to nurse her mother.

So very blessed.

Zander had made good his word—he had made the good better and eased the bad. All her mother's furniture had been moved to Xanos, but the night-time wanderings had stopped and the aggression too. Their daily times on the beach, the salty air and the wonderful food seemed to calm and relax Amanda, or was it the change in her daughter that eased Amanda's mind? For with help and support Charlotte could finally enjoy her mother and help her enjoy the time she had left.

And she wanted more.

As she kissed her mother goodbye and Agira walked her back to the house, Charlotte caught sight of the seaplane coming in to land, and felt the wind whip away selfish tears, for surely when she had so much, when everything she had wished for had come true, it was wrong now to ask for just a little more time.

She watched as the plane landed at the jetty that both brothers now owned. The partnership that had once seemed impossible was a reality now. Old met new in Xanos, the taverna was bustling again with locals, the hotel and restaurants were vibrant, and Ravels was the shining jewel in the island's crown. Charlotte watched as a suited, dark-haired man stepped out, and though he looked like her husband, walked like her husband, to anyone else might well have been her husband, her heart didn't leap, and she knew that it was Nico.

Constantine recognised him too. Charlotte turned as she saw the woman come down to the beach, baby Leo on her hip. She waved to her husband and walked over to join Charlotte, whose heart did tighten now as another suited dark man stepped out, and it was just, just… What was the difference? So many times she tried to pin it down, sure their hair fell differently, one left-handed, the other right-, but from this distance it was impossible to make that out. It was just that her heart told her it was him.

It had told Roula too. For as long as she lived, Charlotte would never forget the smile of disbelief on the older woman's face when she had first seen her grown sons. She had named them immediately—correctly—had taken Zander's tense face in her hands and kissed him, told him how much she had missed him, grief mingling with joy as she held again the son she had been forced to leave behind. Her heart had held more than a three-decade vigil, her love at the centre, and there was no mistaking her heart shone for them. Had Zander had any doubts, Charlotte had watched them fade as he moved towards his mother.

'How do you think it went?' Constantine asked, clearly trying to gauge it, because though both men lived on the island, were in business together, it was still early days. They were two strong personalities and the relationship was still new and, at times, overwhelming, for bruises took time to fade completely.

'Well, they're still talking.' Charlotte smiled, because they were. Nico and Zander walked along the jetty. Zander was nodding at something his brother must have said, and then he looked up and saw her and smiled a smile that crossed the beach like a sunbeam. It warmed her on a cool spring day.

The trips to visit Roula were becoming more regular. Take things slowly, the doctors had warned them for Roula was still very fragile, but the brothers' short visits to Roula were growing longer, and last week, for the first time, the sons had brought their mother for a visit home. It had been hugely emotional watching the fragile woman tremble as she stepped into Nico's home, the home that had once been her father's, watching her stare at the picture on the wall of the babies she had lost.

Only now and then did Charlotte and Constantine join the visits to their mother, but one day, Charlotte was sure, they would bring her home.

'How was she?' Charlotte asked.

'Good,' Zander said. 'Better again. She asked after you.'

'Would you like to come for supper?' Constantine offered, for she was Greek and wanted family at her table. Normally Charlotte left it to Zander to accept or decline, but this time it was Charlotte who answered.

'We'd have loved to, but actually we've got plans tonight.'

They said goodbye. Zander gave little Leo a kiss and then took his wife's hand and walked along the beach toward the development and towards their home.

'What plans do you have for me?' he nudged.

'Oh, I'll think of something.' Charlotte smiled, but her heart wasn't in it and he must have heard the forced lightness to her voice and put his arm around her. 'How was the doctor?' Zander asked. 'How is your mother doing?'

'Good,' Charlotte said. 'He says she is doing well, better than expected.' She stopped walking then. 'I want more time for her…'

'Who knows?' Zander said. 'They did say a couple of months but already she has surpassed that.'

'I want more…'

And Zander heard the plea in her voice that was so rarely there. She asked for nothing and was delighted with everything. For Charlotte to beg, and for something that he could not give, had him turn and pull her into his arms, fighting for words.

'Let's just make each day count,' he settled for. 'Which you already do.'

'I want more!' If she was precise with her wish, maybe it would be answered. 'I want seven months more.' She watched him frown, watched *it* dawn, watched him realise the truth. 'I spoke to the doctor about me as well. We went back to the clinic, he did a test,' Charlotte said. 'A scan.'

'We're having a baby?' He looked at his wife, and he looked into his soul, and he wanted this so badly. He wanted everything that his brother had, not for selfish reasons now, but he had never expected that he would get more.

'We're having twins.'

He put his hand to her stomach, could not believe that it was two hearts that beat in her womb. He knew that things would be different for their babies and he felt the need to share, to spread the good news, to bring things full circle.

'Can we tell him?'

And she nodded with delight, for she did want to be with his family. She had just wanted to tell Zander alone first and would not have been able to hold onto the news for a moment longer.

They walked back along the beach hand in hand, back to the house that had once been Roula's childhood home.

Back to share wonderful news with family.

* * * * *

CLASSIC

Harlequin *Presents*

REQUEST YOUR FREE BOOKS!

◆ Harlequin *Presents*

PASSION GUARANTEED SEDUCTION

2 FREE NOVELS PLUS
2 FREE GIFTS!

Harlequin® Romance

Award-winning author

DONNA ALWARD

*brings you two rough-and-tough
cowboys with hearts of gold.*

CADENCE CREEK
COWBOYS

They're the Rough Diamonds of the West

From the moment Sam Diamond turned up late to her
charity's meeting, placating everyone with a tip of his Stetson
and a lazy smile, Angela Beck knew he was trouble.

Angela is the most stubborn, beautiful woman Sam's ever met
and he'd love to still her sharp tongue with a kiss, but first
he has to get close enough to uncover the complex woman
beneath. And that's something only a real cowboy can do....

THE LAST REAL COWBOY

Available in May.

And look for Tyson Diamond's story,

THE REBEL RANCHER,

coming this June!

Stop The Press! *Crown Prince in Shock Marriage*

When Crown Prince Alessandro of Santina
proposes to paparazzi favorite Allegra Jackson
it promises to be *the* social event of the decade!

Discover all 8 stories in the scandalous
new miniseries THE SANTINA CROWN
from Harlequin Presents®!

***

Enjoy this sneak peek from Penny Jordan's
THE PRICE OF ROYAL DUTY,
book 1 in THE SANTINA CROWN *miniseries.*

"DON'T YOU THINK you're being a tad dramatic?" he
asked her in a wry voice.

"I'm not being dramatic," she defended herself. "Surely
I should have some rights as a person, a human being, some
say in my own fate, instead of having my future decided
for me by my father. To endure marriage to a man who has
simply agreed to marry me because he wants an heir, and to
whom my father has virtually auctioned me off in exchange
for a royal alliance."

"I should have thought such a marriage would suit you,
Sophia. After all, it's well documented that your own chosen lifestyle involves something very similar, when it comes
to bed hopping."

A body blow indeed, and one that drove the blood from
Sophia's face and doubled the pain in her heart. It shouldn't
matter what Ash thought of her. That was not part of her
plan. But still his denunciation of her hurt, and it wasn't one

she could defend herself against. Not without telling him far more than she wanted him to know.

"Then you thought wrong" was all she could permit herself to say. "That is not the kind of marriage I want. I can't bear the thought of this marriage." Her panic and fear were there in her voice; even she could hear it herself, so how much more obvious must it be to Ash?

She must try to stay calm. Not even to Ash could she truly explain the distaste, the loathing, the fear she had of being forced by law to give herself in a marriage bed in the most intimate way possible when… No, that was one secret that she must keep no matter what, just as she had already kept it for so long. "Please, Ash, I'm begging you for your help."

Will Ash discover Sophia's secret?
Find out in THE PRICE OF ROYAL DUTY
by
USA TODAY *bestselling author*
Penny Jordan

Book 1 of THE SANTINA CROWN *miniseries*
available May 2012 from Harlequin Presents®!

Harlequin®

American ★ Romance®

The heartwarming conclusion of

CALLAHAN Cowboys

from fan-favorite author

TINA LEONARD

With five brothers married, Jonas Callahan is under no pressure to tie the knot. But when Sabrina McKinley admits her bouncing baby boy is his, Jonas does everything he can to win over the woman he's loved for years. First the last Callahan bachelor must uncover an important family secret…before he can take the lovely Sabrina down the aisle!

A Callahan Wedding

Available this May wherever books are sold.

www.Harlequin.com